an enchanted place

Jonathan Stedall

Hawthorn Press

An Enchanted Place © 2021 Jonathan Stedall

Jonathan Stedall is hereby identified as the author of this work in accordance with section 77 of the Copyright, Designs and Patent Act, 1988. He asserts and gives notice of his moral right under this Act.

Published by Hawthorn Press, Hawthorn House,
1 Lansdown Lane, Stroud, Gloucestershire, GL5 1BJ, UK
0044 (0) 1453 757040   Email: info@hawthornpress.com

Hawthorn Press
www.hawthornpress.com

Cover illustration © Christine McKechnie
Cover design and typesetting by Lucy Guenot
Typeset in Adobe Garamond Pro and Bodoni
Snail drawing on page 108 © Charlotte Sorapure

Printed by Henry Ling Ltd, The Dorset Press, Dorchester.
Printed on environmentally friendly chlorine-free paper sourced from renewable forest stock.

Every effort has been made to trace the ownership of all copyrighted material. If any omission has been made, please bring this to the publisher's attention so that proper acknowledgement may be given in future editions.

The views expressed in this book are not necessarily those of the publisher.

British Library Cataloguing in Publication Data applied for

ISBN 978-1-912480-46-3
eISBN 978-1-912480-50-0

Dedicated to A. A. Milne, who wrote these words at the conclusion of *The House at Pooh Corner*:

'Come on!'

'Where?' said Pooh.

'Anywhere,' said Christopher Robin.

So they went off together. But wherever they go, and whatever happens to them on the way, in that enchanted place on the top of the Forest a little boy and his Bear will always be playing.

CONTENTS

Chapter One

*In which Bunny organises a meeting,
and Bertie starts work on a poem.*

———————— • ——— • ———— • ————————

The problem about living alone is that there is no one to remind you what you'd promised to do on Tuesday. This was Bertie's morning thought as he paddled about in his slippers looking for clues. Somewhere was a note that he'd written to himself. In the sixty-odd years that they'd been friends – he and this restless, curious being who couldn't stop asking questions about the meaning of life – they had never quite been able to establish a relaxed relationship. Bertie longed to just read his books, stare out of the window and enjoy the forest on his doorstep without being constantly nagged by this other Bertie who couldn't stop wondering why, for instance, trees, flowers, insects and birds seemed to live happily side by side, whereas human beings were so often quarrelling.

At this moment, as he almost tripped over a pile of old newspapers by his back door, he suddenly remembered today's task: a promise to write an article for the local newspaper explaining why people spoke about going for a walk *on* and not *in* their neighbouring forest. In fact the answer was very simple. Most of this so-called forest, apart from one area of woodland, had only a scattering of trees; heather, gorse and bracken covered the remaining 4,000 acres of heathland.

As he settled down to write, little did Bertie know that it was his beloved forest and its very survival that were going to occupy his attention for many months to come. Nor could he know how, through this crisis, he and a group of his friends in the village were about to learn a lot more about each other than they could ever imagine. There certainly wouldn't be much time for quarrelling.

The following morning the storm clouds were already gathering. Bertie's neighbour at The Warren was one of the first people to hear the news on local television. Her voice was sounding more strident than ever. The cut-glass chandelier in the hall would not be the only thing to tremble in the days and weeks to come. Bunny was on the phone, though she had a way of tucking it under her chin so that she could get on with other things at the same time.

'It's appalling,' she said as she picked up her mail from the doormat. 'A bypass across the forest and right through the Five Hundred Acre Wood. We must fight it. Will you join an Action Group I'm forming, Prof? We'll need some people with brains, as well as spears, to lead the protest.'

Bunny was talking to her friend, the Professor, whose family had lived in the village of Hartfield, on the edge of the Ashdown Forest, for nearly as long as hers. Bunny had friends and relations not just in the village, but scattered all over that part of East Sussex and into Kent. She herself was unattached: 'too busy putting the world to rights' was how one of her many friends described her; and certainly not someone to take 'no' for an answer, as certain individuals were soon to discover.

The Professor was busy, too, though he had retired early from his university post and now lived out his comfortable bachelor existence at The Cedars, the family home where he himself had been born. For some time he had been fully occupied in writing a book about late medieval developments in water irrigation. He was also Chairman of the local History Society. Bunny imagined there might be some useful ammunition from that source in the battles that lay ahead.

Despite having no hesitation in approaching such a distinguished member of the community, Bunny did have a somewhat uneasy relationship with her neighbour and had to work hard at not feeling foolish in his company. She knew she was reasonably intelligent, but she tended not to think about life too deeply and was certainly not an intellectual type. Her own education had been sparse, to say the least. As was normal for most young girls of her generation, Bunny had left school at sixteen, whereas her two brothers went on studying well into their twenties. She remembered photographs of them in silver frames on the piano in her parents' home, triumphant in their graduation gowns and holding their silly hats.

Bunny had made up for her lack of formal education by leading an extraordinarily active life – a governor of the local school, coordinator of Meals on Wheels for the surrounding villages, a volunteer at the Citizens Advice Bureau, and queen of the WI. However, a discerning and regular visitor to her house would notice that *The Times*, though prominently displayed on the coffee table beside the latest edition of *Country Life*, had frequently not been opened and clearly not been read.

Bunny was actually christened Elizabeth Margaret, but from a very early age her older brother had called her Bunny, and the name had stuck. In keeping with her brother's image of his lively little sister, she was now busy demolishing a spider's web behind the grandfather clock, while still on the phone to the Professor. It wasn't easy to winkle him out of his cosy study, but she was as single-minded as he was.

'Come over at ten tomorrow morning,' she said, without a thought that the first recruit to her Action Group might actually have other commitments.

The rest of the day was spent assembling what she hoped would be a formidable group of people whose combined skills, knowledge and contacts would put a hasty end to this mad scheme. Traffic through the village wasn't that bad, and to drive a bypass across the forest would be sheer vandalism. And what would happen to the hundreds of Pooh Bear tourists who trekked through the bracken throughout the year in search of their lost childhoods? Hartfield had been the home of A. A. Milne, and the Ashdown Forest was the setting for his stories about 'the bear of very little brain'.

The next person Bunny had decided to approach that morning was her friend Bertie. In fact he was everyone's friend – easy-going, sociable and kind, and someone whose presence on the committee would, she hoped, help to make the others less quarrelsome, less irritated by one another. Although he was, like the Professor, another deep thinker, she didn't find him as forbidding. Perhaps it was simply his tendency to pause as he spoke, as though each word, each thought had to be discovered anew.

Eleven o'clock would be a good time to ask Bertie round, as it was then that he would welcome a cup of coffee and, more importantly, one of her homemade chocolate biscuits. Bertie's visits were often timed to enjoy Bunny's hospitality, but he tended to ignore what he called her 'rabbiting on' about all the dramas in the village; he liked a peaceful life.

Perhaps that's why, when not writing poetry, attending to his beloved bees, or reading books in his search of what he called 'a bigger picture', Bertie most enjoyed the company of his unassuming neighbour Peggy. Walks together on the forest were what they both enjoyed. He did sometimes wonder why Peggy, but never Bunny, was referred to as a 'spinster' by the Professor. And why did people feel so sorry for her? Was it simply her size and her rather quiet voice?

Bunny, meanwhile, had realised that if she did invite Bertie to join the Action Group she would have to ask his friend as well. She was puzzled that he spent so much time with Peggy, who saw danger round every corner. Perhaps he simply didn't notice; he clearly wasn't bothered. However, he was bothered by the announcement of the proposed 'Hartfield Bypass'; the news had travelled fast.

'Bertie, darling, how sweet of you to come round, and at such short notice; just in time for one of your favourite biscuits.' Bunny tried not to be distracted by his muddy shoes; at least they were in keeping with that old baggy pair of trousers that he usually wore.

Bertie seated himself in the most comfortable chair and after making short work of the biscuit, proceeded to read her the first few lines of a poem he'd just started to write about the threat to their precious village and forest. Bertie's poems were not much quoted at poetry festivals – poems that rhyme are considered old-fashioned, the Professor had told him – but they did occasionally feature in the local newspaper.

Why build a road
where heather grows
and people love to roam?

recited Bertie from the crumpled little notebook that he always carried in his back pocket.

Why make a wound
in nature's flesh –
for creatures, it's their home.

As Bertie was reading, Bunny thought to herself how little she cared for poetry. She'd read somewhere that the definition of poetry is the right words in the right order. For her a lot of the words were too obscure, and the order frequently made no sense. She also wondered how anyone had the time to read poetry, let alone to write it. Perhaps that was one of the reasons why dear Bertie enjoys Peggy's company, she thought – someone who listens to his creations and encourages him. Some people need that kind of unconditional support, she decided.

'Lovely!' she said. 'Keep at it, Bertie.' But her attention was already back on the list she was making. It had two columns: one with the names of possible members of her Action Group; the other was an agenda for their first meeting:

1. Introductions.
2. Appoint Secretary.
3. Appoint Treasurer.
4. Suggestions and discussion.
5. Coffee break.
6. Any other business.
7. Date and time of next meeting.

'I've already asked the Professor to join the committee,' she told her thoughtful visitor, who was now gazing out of the window and dreaming up the next line or so of his poem.

'I hope he won't go on and on about the history of road building and the invention of tarmac,' Bertie replied.

'He's knowledgeable, Bertie. We're going to need that sort of expertise; and he's good with the Internet and that sort of thing.'

'What about the Major?' suggested Bertie. 'He'd be surprised to be asked, but he has a certain clout, and he'd keep the lid on our wilder fantasies.'

'You ask him, Bertie. He likes you, as much as he likes anyone. The first meeting is here at my house tomorrow morning at ten.'

'Who else are you considering?' Bertie was slowly starting to take an interest in Bunny's initiative. 'I think Peggy would like to be involved,' he went on, 'and she would worry less about the threat if she had a sense of what's going on and had a role to play.'

'Fine, Bertie. You ask her, too. I'm going to talk to Sheila. Hopefully, she can find someone to babysit for her precious Joey during the meetings.'

Sheila was fairly new to the village – a lone parent from Australia with a somewhat obsessive devotion to her five-year-old son, Joey. The Professor, who was largely unaware of contemporary attitudes to parenthood, referred to her as a 'single mother'. Not quite a scandal, but in his eyes yet another example of how standards had slipped during his lifetime.

Bunny hadn't much liked Sheila when she first arrived in Hartfield – 'that voice, and her rather coarse jokes'. She also felt that dungarees, particularly ones that were emblazoned with slogans like 'When God created man She was just experimenting', were not appropriate for a mature woman and mother to wear. Slowly, however, they had become friends, enjoying long walks together on the forest. Bunny did sometimes wish that Sheila would give Joey a good wallop instead of indulging his every whim. 'Home educated' is how Sheila described the strategy she had adopted for her precious boy; protect the child from the horrors of the world for as long as possible. Bunny had sometimes been tempted to add 'and from the horrors of an over-indulgent parent'.

Peggy was pleased to be asked to join the committee, though was initially concerned that it might involve protests that would become violent. She remembered reading about the opposition to the Okehampton Bypass in Devon, and then the one at Newbury in Berkshire, and what had happened to the people who tied themselves to trees or lay in front of diggers.

Then there was the problem with her eczema when she became stressed. On the other hand she did have quite a lot of time on her hands these days. The sewing group she had started had now folded through lack of interest, and her daily lollipop duty was hardly arduous. Perhaps Bunny would give her some responsibility. She had once learnt shorthand and typing and might be able to brush up those skills.

And so, despite still having slight reservations about this phrase 'Action

Group' – some years ago one of her young nephews had been arrested at a demonstration in London and sent to prison for a month – she felt reassured by her calm and wise friend Bertie, and now trotted along by his side to the far end of the village where the Major, as he was known in the village, lived.

The Major's garden consisted largely of brambles and thistles, the path to his backdoor was overgrown with weeds, and, according to the few people like Bertie and Peggy who had occasionally been invited inside, the house was equally neglected. It was rumoured that he lived largely on Shredded Wheat, but the owner of the village store told Bertie that his friend quite often purchased Marmite and large packets of crisps; also the occasional cigar. Nobody knew if there had ever been a 'Mrs Major' and, if there had, what had happened to her. Sheila had once suggested that she had probably run away to join a circus.

The Major was still in his pyjamas when Bertie and Peggy arrived. As usual he expressed surprise at seeing them, having convinced himself long ago that nobody ever bothered to visit him. In fact he was a much-loved figure in the village, despite his somewhat gloomy approach to life. In his eyes everything was going downhill and had been doing so for years – education, public transport, politics, and Hartfield itself, with the noise of Music Night from the pub on Friday evenings, the closure of the local butcher, a half-empty church, motorbikes, and so it went on. Nevertheless, after some encouraging words from Bertie and Peggy, the Major reluctantly agreed to join the committee, *if* they really wanted him.

'But are you certain you haven't made a mistake, my dear Bertie?' he asked. 'Was it Bunny's idea or yours? She hardly knows me, and I'm not sure what I could contribute. Anyway I expect the whole scheme is already sewn up. Consultations and protests will be allowed to take place, and then the planners will simply do what they intended all along.' By now he was in full swing. 'We think we live in a democracy, but we're too seduced by the glitter of modern life to notice what's really going on.'

To lighten the atmosphere, Peggy suggested that Bertie read the start of his new poem.

'Not now,' was the Major's response. 'I think it's going to rain, so you should be getting home.'

Chapter Two

*In which Sheila gets in a flap,
and the Professor's umbrella goes missing.*

———————•—◆—•———————

Bertie woke up the next morning feeling *pensive*, more pensive than usual. He liked the sound of the word. Pensive was definitely how he was feeling.

The Professor had used that word in his recent lecture to the History Society. It was all Bertie could remember of the evening. Perhaps he'd fallen asleep during some of the talk. To listen to someone for a whole hour, particularly to someone as clever as the Professor, was not the best idea after a good supper.

But there was no time to be pensive this morning. Bunny's Action Group were meeting at ten, and there was breakfast to prepare; then perhaps a quick walk on the forest and a moment to think up some more lines for his new poem. The forest was certainly a good place to go for that, and the idea of noisy traffic tearing past his favourite spots and drowning out those words in his head filled him with horror.

A milder form of horror occurred when Bertie sniffed the milk that he'd forgotten to put back in the fridge yesterday evening, and discovered it had gone off. That meant no cereal for breakfast; he'd have an extra slice of toast to make up for it. And while the kettle boiled he made an effort at tidying some of the books that were scattered all over the floor. The problem was not enough shelf space, though some of the shelves were taken up with treasures he'd found on his walks. The most recent addition was the skeleton of a frog that he'd placed carefully beside a twig he'd found in the shape of a fish. Another challenge was the marks all over the carpet from his muddy shoes; but they weren't yet dry enough to brush away, so that was one less thing to bother about. Anyway some chores can wait until visitors are expected; and, unlike his poem, that sort of muddle was certainly not a priority.

Bertie was already thinking of calling his latest creation 'Action', though he had no idea as yet what sort of action Bunny had in mind. He imagined that the Professor would come up with all sorts of clever ideas, but he had a strong feeling that imagination, humour and our capacity to fantasise were often the most effective weapons against the tyranny of reason. All his life Bertie had thought deeply about human nature, but he felt increasingly at odds with people's tendency to think logically at the expense of their intuition.

These days he tended not to talk or think that much about the past. Increasingly what mattered to him was *now*, and maybe tomorrow. His bees lived in the moment; their kind had done so for millions of years. How wonderful to be a bee, he sometimes thought, though there wouldn't be much time to write poetry. He also imagined that, unlike people, bees never got depressed.

Bertie's low moments – and they had become more frequent in the last year or so – were often prompted by an awareness of how far short he fell from the ideals he loved to read about and that inspired him. In fact he felt that the gap was sometimes so huge that it might be better to simply stop reading those sort of books altogether. Writing poetry and lofty thoughts were all very well, but not if they alienated you from daily life.

Yet what people call daily life is itself a miracle, was his increasing conviction; and nature, above all, was like a mirror in which we can learn not only about ourselves, but also about the great mysteries of existence. Perhaps that should be his next challenge – once the Action Group had triumphed: a poem about why bees never get depressed; angry maybe, but never depressed.

Above all, he reminded himself – as he shoved hard against his back door to close it – he had his friends and his health, and the sun was shining. With these thoughts in mind, and under his 'canopy of blessings' – a phrase that had occurred to him in the night – he felt ready to celebrate another day.

Sheila was in a flap. She wanted to go to Bunny's meeting, but hadn't been able to find anyone to look after Joey at such short notice. She also hadn't been able to get an appointment at the surgery until tomorrow afternoon and was concerned about the spot that had appeared on Joey's back. It was probably the reason he'd refused to eat his breakfast, even though she'd offered him some sugar on his cereal as a treat. She was worried, too, that the pullover he'd been wearing perhaps wasn't made from pure wool, despite what it said on the label.

Sheila had only lived in Hartfield for just over a year, and she was still trying to adjust to English village life. In the outback of Australia where she'd grown up – her parents had emigrated there when she was two years old – people said what they thought, and often in pretty fruity language. In Hartfield she'd already offended the vicar by calling him 'mate'. 'Good onya, mate' is what she'd actually said as she saw him bicycling through the rain for early morning Communion. Likewise the Professor was none too pleased at being referred to as 'a great bloke'. Fortunately, no one had told the Major that Sheila referred to him as 'the wombat' because of his prominent front teeth.

Despite these clangers, Sheila was still keen to be part of village life, and Bunny's Action Group would be an excellent platform from which to start making a contribution. Unfortunately, she would have to take Joey to this first meeting, but with a promise that if he misbehaved – which in her eyes he rarely did – they would leave.

But there was more to Sheila than just wisecracks. She, too, had her masks, but underneath took a real interest in what makes people tick. At first she'd experienced Bunny as rather a snob, with her posh house and her account at Harrods; but, gradually getting to know her better, she'd understood how someone with all that self-confidence could also be vulnerable. The ice first broke when Bunny came across Sheila in tears outside the Post Office. Over a cup of coffee in her kitchen, Bunny then let slip that she'd once been engaged, but was jilted just one week before the wedding. It was through the previously unspoken realm of their feelings of insecurity that they had slowly forged a bond.

Peggy arrived at Bunny's house ten minutes early. She always hated to be late for anything, and perhaps she'd be able to help with moving the chairs or laying a tray for the coffee break. She was wearing a cameo broach that had belonged to her grandmother and which she kept for special occasions.

Like everyone else, Peggy had received a copy of the agenda through her letterbox the previous evening. Since then she'd been wondering if they'd consider her for the role of Secretary, but she was frightened at the idea of having to deal with the Professor on her own. In fact she didn't really feel confident enough to do more than take down notes, but maybe that would be useful.

Sheila turned up alone – a neighbour had kindly stepped in to keep an eye on Joey – just as Peggy was taking off her coat and scarf. Although it was still September, the cautious Peggy knew how treacherous the autumn weather could be and was taking no chances. She greeted Sheila nervously and asked after Joey. Earlier in the year she'd tried to help him retrieve some frog spawn from the village pond, but had fallen in. Ever since he'd always called her Froggy, but not to her face.

The Professor arrived at ten o'clock exactly, dressed as always in a crumpled tweed suit and wearing a rather flashy tie. Sheila later remarked to Bunny that the flash was probably some of his breakfast.

The Major and Bertie were ten minutes late owing to the fact that the Major had waved down a speeding car in the village and was only rescued from what the police would call 'an incident' by the reassuring presence of Bertie.

The meeting then got off to a speedy start; with Bunny in charge it could hardly have been otherwise. As everyone knew each other the Introductions were unnecessary. It was quickly agreed that Bunny should be the Secretary, and the word 'Chairperson' was added beside her name. Peggy was relieved rather than disappointed. Already she'd started to feel out of place and was longing for a quiet walk with Bertie that afternoon. She also couldn't stop worrying about a form that the Council had sent her to fill in, and desperately needed his advice. It was hard to think about anything else.

Sheila agreed to be the Treasurer, as she had once worked for a few months in a bank in Melbourne after leaving university. No one knew – not even Bunny – that it was there, in the vault after the bank closed, that a brief affair with the night watchman had been the invitation for Joey to come into the world.

Next came the Suggestions and Discussion, but already Bertie was longing for the coffee break. It seemed to him that at meetings, in particular, people tended to use ten words when maybe two or three would do; they also listened to each other even less than usual.

The Major repeated his forecast that the planned bypass would eventually go ahead, however much the locals protested. Bunny said that they shouldn't underestimate the power of local opinion. The Professor undertook to set up a website and also to research the history of other bypass protests, and if necessary to contact key activists through the Internet for advice about tactics.

Next it was agreed that Bertie would take on the publicity, producing leaflets and writing to the local papers. Bunny and the Professor both very tactfully tried to emphasise the value of clear, simple prose as against poetry. Peggy volunteered to help him, and Bunny was relieved that Peggy had found herself a role. Bunny herself would follow up her contacts in the Parish Council. Sheila meanwhile would investigate social media options.

It was then that the Professor brought up the subject of Sir Christopher, who was somewhat of a legend in Hartfield. Christopher had grown up in the village, and older residents like Bertie and Peggy, the Major, Bunny and the Professor himself had known him well. However, some years ago he had moved to London and now had a high-powered job at the Home Office. He seldom came back to Hartfield, but the Professor felt that 'for old time's sake' their friend might be prepared to pull a few strings in Whitehall and particularly at the Department of Transport. Bunny's initial instinct was that they should be prepared to fight the battle on their own; moreover, getting involved in Whitehall politics would be just another layer of bureaucracy that they could do without. The prospect of the East Sussex County Council was daunting enough. Bertie, who was now paying attention, agreed with her, but he was particularly fond of Christopher and said it was worth a try and that he would write a letter himself.

None of them, apart from the Major, had any real sense that a battle of this magnitude was probably already being fought out in the corridors of power, irrespective of how many marches took place, and however many leaflets were distributed and articles written. Nonetheless, at the back of Bertie's mind there lingered the story of David and Goliath, and with it his sense that in all good stories the giant is eventually defeated.

The Coffee Break was a jolly affair until the phone rang and Joey's babysitter, obviously close to tears, begged Sheila to come home as soon as possible. Any Other Business then consisted of comforting Sheila and calming down the Major, who was convinced that someone had stolen his umbrella.

The next meeting was fixed for the following Wednesday at 8 p.m. Bertie hoped that Bunny might offer to give him supper beforehand, perhaps in return for a pot of honey. He seldom ate with Peggy, as her diet was eccentric in the extreme. She frequently made soup from her leftovers, including potato skins and orange peel. She also had a habit of eating her apple cores, though at least without the stalks. Most endearing of all, in Bertie's eyes, was her love of that Swiss cheese with holes in it. Her godmother had told her when she was a young girl that the holes tasted best of all, and she still believed it.

Chapter Three

In which Sheila takes in a lodger,
and the Major makes a joke.

———◆———

As the daylight hours began to decrease and the forest slowly changed into its autumn colours, blissfully unaware of the threat it faced, members of the Action Group continued to go about their lives much as before.

Some were more concerned than others about what might lie ahead, but there were other distractions that also called for attention; for example the winter fuel needed ordering. Bertie preferred logs, but Peggy liked coal because it gave out more heat. The Major was devoted to his ancient electric fire, despite the escalating cost of his electricity bill; but he now started to worry about winter hazards like burst pipes and blocked gutters. Peggy's worry was the prospect of being blocked in by snow, and not being able to get to the shops, even though she lived in the heart of the village. Thus every autumn she made a habit of stocking up with tins of food and plenty of frozen vegetables.

Meanwhile the Professor bought his first packet of crumpets, which reminded him of comfortable afternoons in the Senior Common Room. Sheila tried unsuccessfully to interest Joey in Victoria plums; apparently he didn't like the stones. At the far end of the village Bertie was busy putting his bees to bed for the winter.

A few days after that first meeting at her house, Bunny learned from Peggy, who'd heard it from Bertie, that Sheila had taken in a lodger. Bouncer, as he liked to be called, was an actor and had recently been in a television series, set in a supermarket, that nobody seemed to have seen. Tired of living in London, he'd decided to explore their part of East Sussex which, despite its very traditional appearance, was – so he'd heard – a magnet for people considered to be somewhat alternative.

Bouncer was large and friendly, so Bunny was told, had a loud voice, was full of stories and wore colourful clothes, including striped shirts with socks to match. Bunny didn't like the sound of him at all; not someone who would fit comfortably into village life.

For Sheila, however, the extra cash would be helpful and would supplement the small allowance that the Australian night watchman occasionally sent her. Thankfully, her lodger seemed prepared to muck in with her somewhat erratic routine, though he turned out to be quite a fussy eater. At least her home was a lot nicer than most theatrical digs, thought Sheila, despite the fact that there was no theatre anywhere near. The Village Hall was largely used by the WI, the History Society and a Weight Watchers group.

In fact Sheila took great pride in her home, and in her vegetable garden, and was in the midst of spring-cleaning when Bouncer had first knocked on her door. When Peggy had politely remarked the following day that spring-cleaning was usually done in the spring and not in September, Sheila responded by saying that it was spring in Australia.

Since the first meeting of the Action Group, the Professor had been busy on the Internet and had already come up with some potentially helpful information about protests against the Newbury Bypass nearly thirty years ago. Apparently the proposed route was delayed and nearly thrown out, not only because of the need to fell nearly 10,000 mature trees, but because of the discovery of a colony of rare snails on the site. The Professor was also intrigued to find out that these minute creatures, known as Desmoulin's whorl snails, were named in honour of the nineteenth-century French naturalist Charles des Moulins. The whorl snail is, as he carefully noted down, 'a species of minute air-breathing land snail, a terrestrial pulmonate gastropod mollusc or micromollusc in the family of Ver- tiginidae, with the scientific name *Vertigo moulininsiana*'.

Even more interesting to the Professor was that, according to a recent report to the European Commission in accordance with the Habitats Directive, whorls are a critically endangered species in the Czech Republic, and in Poland and Spain; they are possibly extinct in Algeria.

Having spent a further hour or so researching detailed descriptions of whorls, the Professor decided to take this information to the next meeting of the Action Group, along with some important news about what eventually hap- pened at Newbury.

Apart from preparing his bees for winter, and rather than thinking too deeply about the threat of a bypass across his beloved forest, Bertie had spent much of his time since the first meeting of the Action Group in reading and trying to understand his new book about the two very different ways that people try to understand the world.

The first path, it was suggested, was through analysis. It was how the Professor's mind seemed to function, with an emphasis on logic and on differ- entiation and classification. Bertie, on the other hand, saw himself largely in the second camp, which was primarily guided by intuition and involved the imagination and a tendency to see things from a holistic point of view. In this sense he felt an affinity with those whom the Church had traditionally called 'contemplatives'. He couldn't imagine the Professor gazing out of the window for long periods of time, or wanting to write poetry; but he, on the other hand, recognised how bewildered he was by much modern technology, and by computers in particular. Reading *In the Shadow of the Machine* was helping him to understand this polarity in human nature and the need for balance.

On the Saturday after the meeting, Bertie and Peggy called by to see the Major again, as it was at weekends that their friend tended to feel particularly melancholic and in need of cheering up.

'Have they started digging yet?' he asked them as soon as he opened the door. This time he was fully dressed, but Peggy noticed that his socks didn't match and that his grey cardigan was done up incorrectly, giving him a somewhat lopsided appearance.

'Digging what?' asked Bertie.

'The bypass, of course. Autumn is a good time to cut down trees, once they start shedding their leaves.'

Clearly the Major held out little hope of preventing what he ironically called 'progress'. Rather than trying to argue, Bertie and Peggy decided to have a go at his kitchen. Washing-up tended to pile up until he'd run out of clean mugs and plates, and they liked the idea of a cup of tea. This involved a hazardous expedition to the cupboard in his porch which he called 'the larder'.

The Major was a contemplative of sorts, thought Bertie, although his temperament was such that everything he contemplated was, in his eyes, sad and hopeless. The mystery of his missing umbrella still haunted him. Peggy tried to make their friend smile by talking about the arrival of Bouncer in the village and about Bunny's aversion to people who were, in her words, too theatrical. The Major didn't smile, but he did say that he liked plays, especially Shakespeare's tragedies. Peggy had only ever seen *The Mousetrap* and *The Sound of Music*, so suddenly felt rather out of her depth. Bertie tried to rescue the situation by asking the Major if he'd ever acted.

'At school once,' he replied, 'in a Nativity Play; and guess who was given the part of Mary and Joseph's donkey!'

Now he did smile, just very briefly, but for Bertie it was as though the sun had suddenly come out, and for a moment he even imagined the angels in heaven were clapping.

Maybe a visit from Bouncer would do the Major good, he thought. Despite being so loud and cheerful, an actor of Bouncer's vintage was bound to have acted in a tragedy or two, and he probably had some hilarious backstage stories that might make even the Major laugh.

Peggy meanwhile had started to help their host to sort out his laundry, which was spread out all the way up the stairs. She had no close family of her own and liked to help her friends in the village whenever the occasion arose. She even offered to have a go at his ironing, but he said very firmly that he didn't believe in ironing; it was unnecessary, and a waste of electricity.

The next day Bertie decided that it was time to meet Bouncer and to help him feel welcome in the village. He was sure that Bunny's instinctive hostility was unjustified; she simply didn't like strangers, particularly ones who looked and behaved differently.

Bertie, too, liked his routine, and also had a fairly conventional approach to things like clothes. At this time of year all that mattered was something warm that didn't have any holes in it. A few months ago Peggy had patched his favourite pullover, but he'd recently discovered a new hole. Nevertheless he also liked variety and surprises, and was thus rather intrigued by the idea of striped shirts with socks to match. As a goodwill gesture he decided to take round a jar of his honey.

Unlike most modern beekeepers, Bertie only took the surplus honey from his hives in the spring and never gave his bees sugar syrup as a second-rate substitute. Years ago he'd read that robbing bees of too much of their honey had, over the past hundred years or so, gradually weakened their immune system, making them vulnerable to attack by various parasites and diseases; previously they had been strong and healthy enough to keep these things at bay. Bertie enjoyed and was very proud of his honey, but didn't want to be a thief. The honey belonged to the bees; they worked hard to make it, and needed it to survive over the winter. If, at the start of summer, there was some to spare he gratefully helped himself.

'This is how our ancestors behaved,' he had told Peggy on one of their walks. 'They lived as partners with nature and not as exploiters.'

Peggy had wondered whether all the talk about climate change was the same problem. People had simply become too greedy. Last year someone had tried to persuade her to have solar panels fitted on her cottage roof, but she'd refused. They look so ugly, she thought. Maybe she should think again, but try to find some that looked more like tiles and not like television screens.

After that conversation with Bertie, it had also occurred to her that people, and not just bees, were having the same problems with their health through a weakened immune system. Everyone knew that our crazy, stressful lives, with not enough exercise, the wrong sort of food and too many antibiotics, are bad for us. Like the bees, she thought, we too have become more vulnerable to diseases and illness.

The visit to meet Bouncer was a success, though Peggy did find him a bit too large and loud. 'Over the top' had been one of Sheila's more restrained comments.

He accepted the honey enthusiastically by hugging them both and, on hearing about yesterday's conversation with the Major, expressed an interest in meeting him. However, he wasn't able to make any definite arrangements, as he was waiting for a call from his agent. Peggy asked him if he'd ever met anyone famous.

'*I'm* famous,' he said with a roar of laughter, and gave her another big hug, much to the amusement of Joey.

Bertie decided there and then that a visit to the Major was maybe not such a good idea – at least not for a while.

Meanwhile, at the other end of the village, Bunny was accumulating all sorts of impenetrable information from the District and County Councils about public enquiries, while the Professor – now settled comfortably in his armchair – had sent off to Blackwell's in Oxford for *An Illustrated Guide to Snails* in two volumes.

When Bertie finally got home from his meeting with Bouncer he suddenly remembered the letter he'd promised to write to his old friend Christopher in London, but decided to leave it until the morning. He was too tired to read any more of his new book, so instead he sat peacefully by his fire and thought about nothing but the beautiful pattern made by the burning logs.

Chapter Four

*In which Bunny takes against Bouncer,
and a hunt for whorls is proposed.*

———————•———•———

Bertie was rather dreading the next meeting of the Action Group, partly because he would have nothing to report about Christopher's response to the crisis, since the letter he had promised to send had only been posted two days ago. As there was no invitation to supper from Bunny, he cooked himself a poached egg on toast and took an apple to eat on the way to the meeting.

At the sight of Bunny's flip chart he almost fell asleep on the spot, but was rapidly brought down to earth by an extravagant greeting from Bouncer. Sheila had invited her lodger to the meeting at the last minute, and without consulting Bunny. She thought it would be a good opportunity for them to meet, but it very soon became clear that it was a mistake, not least because of Bouncer's tendency to hog the limelight. On this occasion that role belonged to Bunny, or so she thought.

Another reason that Sheila had invited him to join them was that she'd been impressed by all the important people that he seemed to know, often referring to them as friends. Before the meeting started she tried to explain to Bunny that this wider circle of contacts might be useful in the weeks and months ahead, but it was too late. As Bouncer held forth to the Professor, and to anyone else who might be interested, about his time at the National, the Chairperson was soon in no mood to listen to other people's initiatives.

Meanwhile the Major, as Bertie had anticipated, didn't take to the newcomer's loud voice and even louder laugh. Peggy, too, retreated into her shell with her cup of coffee, unwilling to engage with this inquisitive and restless stranger who was constantly running his hand through his mop of thick, black hair.

'Some Asian blood there, if you ask me,' was Bunny's remark to the Professor later that evening.

Although Sheila was regretting her decision to bring Bouncer along, even before the actual meeting started, she knew that he meant well and was genuinely friendly; and she hoped that the others would eventually recognise the fact.

Despite this unfortunate start to the evening, Bunny was soon in full swing, explaining to everyone what she'd discovered about the ins and outs of the legal procedures that lay ahead. She had spoken to someone at the County Council, someone else at the Department of Transport, and was trying to make contact with Natural England; a Public Consultation was in the pipeline. But she'd also been advised by a planning inspector she knew that if the locals could come up with enough significant objections, then the whole scheme could possibly be nipped in the bud. Some of the information that she now shared with them, along with her diagrams and graphs, was hard to follow and somewhat tedious, and Bertie felt in danger of nodding off.

Bunny had also come across rumours that the whole bypass scheme was linked to plans for the creation of over five hundred new homes between Hart-field and Tunbridge Wells. 'Not in my backyard' was the unanimous response of all those present, though it did occur to Bertie, and secretly even to Bunny, that people had to live somewhere. Bunny's extended family were spread out all over the surrounding area, but some of the younger members were finding it hard to get on the housing ladder and felt more and more trapped in a hole that was not of their own making.

The meeting started to brighten up – initially at least – when the Professor came to give his report on the protests over the Newbury Bypass back in the nineties, and on the drama created by the discovery of this colony of very rare snails called whorls.

Bunny's flip chart then gave him ample opportunity to elaborate on every aspect of these obscure and minute creatures, but, after ten minutes or so of information about the history and the habitat of whorls, some people's attention began to flag.

These particular snails liked to live in 'calcareous wetlands', the Professor told them. What on earth is that? wondered Bertie as *his* thoughts, too, began to wander. Uppermost in his mind was the wish that he'd had *two* poached eggs for supper, and maybe a decent pudding to follow. At least he was awake, unlike the Major. Bouncer, too, felt himself losing the plot and began to get restless.

But then the proceedings took an interesting and unexpected turn; even the Major woke up, and Bertie stopped thinking about poached eggs. What the Professor was telling them was that it was finally agreed that, instead of altering the route of the Newbury Bypass to avoid the snails, the whole colony would be moved – at the contractor's expense – to another piece of boggy land three miles away. *But* it was discovered four years later that the colony had died out; they hadn't survived the move.

'Perhaps they tried to go back to their original home', suggested Peggy, 'and got run over on the new road. Lots of creatures have that instinct.' She felt proud at last to have made a contribution.

But something far more important than the migratory habits of snails occurred to several members of the group after hearing about the sad demise of the Newbury whorls. It was Bertie who was the first to put it into words, despite the fact that the Professor was still in full flood.

'Maybe there are some Desmoulin's whorl snails on the Ashdown Forest,' Bertie piped up.

Bouncer's reaction to Bertie's suggestion – the first time he'd spoken at the meeting – was delivered with characteristic theatricality: 'Bye-bye bypass!' It was a phrase that Bertie immediately scribbled down in his notebook for possible inclusion in his poem.

And so by the end of the meeting there was suddenly a real and exciting plan; and for the members of the Action Group it meant that they could start to live up to their name, not just by talking and writing letters, but also through *action*. If a colony of whorl snails was living somewhere along the proposed route of the bypass, then moving them would no longer be an option. But someone had to find them.

It was therefore decided that they would immediately begin a hunt on the forest for whorls, with Bertie in charge. Even the Major indicated that he would be up for the occasional stroll; and Peggy had already started to dream that she would be the one who found the first snail.

Bouncer assured them all that he had particularly good eyesight, having once done a course in repairing clocks and watches. He'd long been aware that most actors needed a second string to their bow, though he had soon found that for him that particular skill was too finicky and sedentary.

Sheila added that Joey was brilliant at finding ants and earwigs in the garden and might also be helpful. She failed to mention what tortures he then inflicted on them.

The Professor was secretly proud that it was his research that had prompted this initiative, though the thought of actual whorl snails on their doorstep had only fleetingly occurred to him. Facts were what he liked, and certainly not long walks in the wind and rain, let alone crawling on hands and knees among the bracken and mud.

And it was indeed in the mud, and in damp and boggy places, that whorls liked to live. The Professor's research had also revealed the following: whorl snails are about two to three millimetres long (which meant very little to those like Bertie and Peggy who still thought in feet and inches); their shells are yellowish or brownish and translucent; and they have four to seven fairly prominent teeth, which made Sheila worry for a moment that Joey might get bitten.

When Peggy got home from the meeting she made herself a cup of cocoa and then fell asleep in her armchair. She woke around midnight, having dreamt about a whorl that was two to three *feet* long and had a lot more than seven teeth.

Two days later Bertie received a handwritten note from Sir Christopher in which he promised to talk to one or two of his contacts in Whitehall, and meanwhile sent everyone his best wishes for their campaign. Bertie hadn't really expected his busy and important friend to come tearing down to Sussex on the next train, but he also sensed from the note how little people really care about problems that are not on their own doorstep. But he wasn't upset by this realisation. He decided to go for a walk.

He knew it was ten o'clock without looking at his watch. In fact his watch was still on the table by his bed. For the past month or so he'd been experimenting at guessing the time and had found that the more he just guessed without thinking about it too much, the more accurate he became. However, he didn't yet risk relying on this new skill when something like a meeting of the Action Group was looming. Bunny didn't like people being late, and everyone was rather scared of bossy Bunny.

Bertie's thoughts about time had been prompted by a chapter in his new book which described the invention of the first clocks nearly seven centuries ago. He'd been interested to learn that, before then, people's experience of time was determined by what was taking place in the sky and in nature; and there was also no sense that hours should be of equal length throughout the year. But with the development of the kind of logical thinking that Bertie recognised the Professor did so well, and as people gradually became onlookers rather than participants in the natural world around them, they also became more and more skilled in making not just clocks, but machines of ever-greater complexity.

The first clocks, so Bertie read, were celestial clocks that could accurately mirror the movements of the sun, moon and planets. Then gradually, and perhaps inevitably, people began to see the universe itself as a great machine – a clock, in fact – no longer alive and permeated by supernatural beings.

This ability to think logically at the expense of intuitive awareness has come, so the book suggested, at a certain cost. It was this cost that Bertie, in his own quiet way, was increasingly aware of and concerned about. Above all, it was the attitude that nature could be manipulated for our convenience that worried him most of all. It was why he wrote poetry; why he tried not to exploit his bees; and why he treasured his moments of solitude on the forest.

To build a bypass you had to think clearly and logically; that was obvious. But to stop a bypass being built, he realised, you had to think intuitively and imaginatively. Reason tells us that something as small and insignificant as a snail can simply be bulldozed out of the way. But Bertie also knew very well that being human involves the heart as well as the head. Both would be needed in the battles ahead.

CHAPTER FIVE

*In which the Professor upsets Bertie,
and Peggy comes up with some facts and figures.*

'I thought you might be interested in these,' said the Professor as he thrust a couple of newspaper articles in Bertie's direction.

It was three days since the meeting of the Action Group, and Bertie had been invited to call by at The Cedars for a chat. In fact the Professor knew perfectly well that the articles would upset rather than interest his friend, but he was constantly irritated by people like Bertie who, in his eyes, always tended to take a suspicious view of the latest scientific discoveries and developments. 'Dreamers stuck in the past and fearful of change' was how he saw them.

As the Professor expected, Bertie read the two articles with alarm; but above all he was overcome by a feeling of deep sadness. Some scientists in the Netherlands, so it was reported, were in the process of developing bee-like drones, capable of pollinating plants in preparation for the day when real-life insects will have largely died out owing to the excessive use of pesticides.

The other article was about the breeding of chemically resistant bees. In Bertie's mind this idea totally ignored the real problem. The sick bees were a warning. The real problem was our lack of understanding of and respect for the subtle interconnectedness of all living things.

As Bertie finally looked up from reading, he told the Professor that he was reminded of the traditional role of the canary in the coal mine, whose silence was a warning of toxic fumes. The approach now advocated by these scientists would be similar to replacing the dead canary with another canary.

'Or simply fitting the canary with a gas mask,' he added.

The Professor didn't smile as Bertie had hoped he might.

'The world doesn't need artificial or chemically resistant bees,' Bertie continued. 'It needs farming practices that don't harm bees.'

The Professor was not remotely convinced.

'My dear Bertie, how are we going to feed the world's growing population if we don't adopt new and more efficient ways of doing things.' It was the familiar argument addressed to conservationists like Bertie.

'Never mind what it is that we're actually eating,' was Bertie's immediate thought, but he knew that it was hopeless to continue the conversation. Instead he looked out of the window and, for a moment and as so often before, felt a profound concern for the plants and insects, the birds and the butterflies that he loved so much and on which we all depend; a concern for their struggle to stay healthy and to survive in a world that is increasingly polluted by us human beings.

He wondered, too, how someone like the Professor could reconcile what he absorbed every Sunday in church with his basically mechanistic picture of nature and of life in general. No clue was forthcoming.

Having said his bit on behalf of progress, the Professor filed away the two articles and then wound up the clock on his mantelpiece. Bertie liked the atmosphere in the Professor's study, with its comfortable leather armchairs, books arranged neatly on solid oak shelves, and the view onto the garden and the magnificent old cedar tree that shielded it from the neighbouring houses.

Bertie sometimes wished that he could live in such ordered surroundings, but he never seemed to have time to make the changes he could envisage. Perhaps it was just a question of priorities.

'Any news about the next meeting?' asked the Professor as he settled back in his armchair.

'Bunny said she'd let us know as soon as her plans for the week fell into place. Meanwhile I'm thinking of organising our first whorl hunt. Are you still up for it?'

Bertie was starting to feel his cheerful self again, particularly at the thought of such a challenging adventure.

'Of course,' said the Professor, relieved that the argument – an argument that he'd provoked – was seemingly forgotten.

But these things aren't forgotten, Bertie would later tell Peggy. 'All we can do', he said to her, 'is to try and respect the fact that everyone is entitled to their own opinion, and yet to still care about them, even if we don't agree with them. Meanwhile, any plea to the Prof on behalf of the ecosystem is like water off a duck's back.'

'But we're not ducks,' was Peggy's witty response.

Bertie smiled at the thought of their learned friend all covered with feathers.

'But he *has* got an amazing brain,' Peggy added.

'Yes, I know,' said Bertie. 'I sometimes think it's why he never understands anything!'

Peggy laughed, but what touched her most of all was Bertie's next remark as they clambered through the wet autumn heather, up towards their favourite viewpoint on the forest.

'Human beings are essentially well-meaning,' he said between puffs, 'but we are all frail and essentially in the dark; no wonder we do and say such stupid things. By the way, I'm sure I recognised the Major's umbrella in the Professor's hall as I was leaving, but I didn't like to say anything.'

Bunny meanwhile was busy planning the next meeting of the Action Group, but uppermost in her mind was how to exclude Bouncer without causing too much offence. He irritated her intensely. If it hadn't been for Sheila's inappropriate initiative in bringing him along to the last meeting, he would never have been involved. He was new to the village, knew hardly anyone and had probably never set foot on the forest.

Her plan was to take advantage of Bouncer's forthcoming appointment with his agent in London – apparently it might also involve an audition – which she learned from Sheila had now been settled for Thursday. She wrote a quick note to everyone (and an email to the Professor) apologising for the short notice and saying that Thursday at noon was the only day and time she could manage this week and that it was essential to meet as soon as possible, as she had some important news to share.

Relieved and energised by her cunning plan, Bunny now turned her attention to the WI and the choice of their first speaker in the New Year. One suggestion had been a woman whose campaign to sabotage fox hunting had landed her in prison on three occasions. As many of the members of the WI whom Bunny knew tended to be more interested in hunting for bargains in the sales in Tunbridge Wells, or even better in Brighton, than in the fate of an animal that hardly any of them had ever even seen, she decided it would be better to go for the jam and chutney expert from Lewes. Further encouraged by yet another decision, she set off for her weekly stint at the Citizens Advice Bureau.

The following day found several, but not all, members of the Action Group assembled at Bertie's house for their first expedition. Peggy had been the first to arrive, armed with two thermoses of coffee, some plastic cups and a packet of digestive biscuits, all tucked into the same satchel that she'd had since childhood.

The Professor had phoned to say he was developing a cold, but had supplied each of them with an illustrated printout of the whorl snail in all its glory. Bunny had also apologised for her absence, owing to an unexpected call from a relative who was unwell.

The Major was there, much to everyone's surprise, and dressed as though they were going on a trip to the African jungle. For safety's sake he'd also brought along a torch, an extra-thick pair of gardening gloves, a compass and whistle and his pair of binoculars. Sheila, who arrived last, together with Bouncer and Joey, said a magnifying glass might have been more useful – but not loud enough for the Major to hear.

Bertie had obtained a map outlining the proposed bypass from his contact at the local newspaper, and he had brought along a plastic bag just in case they found a whorl or two on their very first walk. The plan was to start by exploring the marshy areas along the route, starting from the western end.

Having been a volunteer warden when she first came to live in Hartfield, Peggy knew quite a lot of facts about the forest: that it was an Area of Outstanding Natural Beauty, a former medieval hunting forest, a Site of Special Scientific Interest and a Special Protection Area. Quite a lot of 'specials', she thought, but clearly not enough to keep the developers at bay.

Bertie, in contrast, simply knew how the forest looked and felt, the scents and the colours, and above all its welcoming feel, whether it was morning or afternoon, in mist or in sunshine, and whatever the month; he even loved it in the rain.

With no Professor to intimidate her, Peggy felt confident to tell Bouncer, the newcomer, about this great open space on their doorstep. She was also relieved that he didn't seem quite so large when out of doors and in such a wonderful setting. In fact he almost seemed dwarfed by it, she later confided to Bertie.

'More than half the forest is heathland, and the rest woodland,' Peggy told her enthusiastic companion in one of the few moments when he slowed down. Most of the time he was bounding on ahead and chasing little Joey in a wild game of hide-and-seek.

'It's why we say *on* the forest and not *in*, because there's far more heathland than trees. The bracken is a problem, though, as it tends to take over.'

'I love it,' said Bouncer. 'I love the colour; it's like the leaves, almost more beautiful when it's dying.'

'In the past the commoners used it as bedding for their livestock,' she told him. 'Hardly any of them now exist. All people keep nowadays are dogs and cats.'

'And horses and guinea pigs,' volunteered Joey, who'd been listening to the conversation.

Peggy was now in full stride, and pleased that people seemed interested in what she was saying.

'The woodland, too, needs controlling,' she went on. 'It tends to encroach on the heathland because of the decline in grazing.'

Sheila then chipped in with a phrase that had amused her in some guidebook she'd read: 'Exotic plant encroachment', it had said, 'was another threat to the forest.'

'They mean rhododendrons,' said Peggy.

'Am I "an exotic encroachment" on your green and pleasant land?'

asked their playful Aussie friend. Before anyone could respond, she sped off
to rescue Joey, who had wandered away on his own and fallen flat on his face
in the heather.

'He's just tripped in a rabbit hole,' called out Bouncer, who was fast
getting used to Sheila's anxiety regarding Joey's every step in life. Too many
pavements these days, and not enough hazards, he thought as he remembered
his own childhood in a remote village in Yorkshire, and walking two miles across
fields to school.

By this time they had reached a low-lying area where there were several ponds,
which, according to Peggy, were home to great crested newts and in the summer to dragonflies and to a small and rare damselfly. But nobody was listening
properly to her facts and figures any more. All were already on their hands and
knees in search of something much more interesting than newts and dragonflies. Would they find whorls among the damp grass and reeds that bordered
the ponds?

Even the Major was no longer quite vertical, thanks to his shooting stick
that had been a present from Bertie and Peggy for his seventieth birthday. Sheila
couldn't quite concentrate on the hunt, as she was terrified that Joey would fall
into one of the ponds. Despite being brought up in the wilds of Australia she
was also in constant fear of adders, she confided in Bouncer.

'With an invasion of this magnitude,' he teased her, 'they've probably
all moved forest!'

Joey, meanwhile, was thrilled to have found a giant spider and was
about to remove its legs when Bouncer came to its rescue.

'It's called a raft spider,' said Peggy, who was kneeling beside them and
rather wishing that she'd brought a warmer pair of socks. 'It's the largest spider
there is, and quite rare.'

'There are bigger ones in the jungle,' said Joey, who'd seen a programme
about insects on television.

'It will probably soon be extinct,' mumbled the Major. 'Much like
everything else of real interest,' he quietly added.

Meanwhile Bertie had found a comfortable seat on what he assumed was an
abandoned anthill. Some lines of poetry had occurred to him, and he wanted to
write them down. His memory wasn't quite so good these days, though he did
suddenly remember Peggy's coffee and biscuits.

A pause in the hunt was generally welcomed, before they moved on to
the next pond. Sheila had already begun to wonder whether whorls really would
be found on the Ashdown Forest. Newbury was at least a hundred miles away,

and the other statistics that the Professor had come up with could be years out of date; and maybe those rare snails discovered in Berkshire were the last of the species in England.

The Major, meanwhile, had arrived at much the same thought, and his starting to feel cold had increased his pessimism. Desmoulin's whorl snails, he thought – like raft spiders and hedgehogs and red squirrels – would soon exist only in the Natural History Museum. So much of the England that he had known as a child had disappeared, and he was sometimes quietly relieved by the thought that he wouldn't live long enough to witness the countryside's final destruction.

Sheila and Peggy were, in their different ways, too anxious to philosophise or speculate. Bouncer, too, tended to live in the moment, but happily so; it was why, in the eyes of many, he was such good company.

Bertie, meanwhile – despite an uncomfortable itching in his trousers – remained optimistic. Despite his occasional bouts of depression, he was happy to live most days with the feeling that life could and indeed does get better, but only if people work to help it along. If you believed strongly enough that in time a whorl snail would appear, then such a creature would eventually oblige; that was what he liked to think. And if Peggy's caution was balanced by Bouncer's enthusiasm, and if the Professor's intellect, Bunny's energy and Sheila's humour were all harmoniously combined, then the Major's pessimism – although it helped to keep them all grounded – would finally not be allowed to triumph.

It was typical of Bertie's approach to life that he gave no thought to the vital role that he himself played in the lives of his friends and neighbours.

Chapter Six

In which Bertie and Bouncer discuss bees,
and Bunny's cunning plan backfires.

—————— · ✦ · ——————

A couple of days after the unsuccessful hunt for whorls, Bouncer knocked on Bertie's door just as his new friend was finishing breakfast.

'Come in!' called Bertie cheerily. 'Like a cup of coffee?'

'No thanks,' said his guest, who appeared somewhat subdued. 'I actually wondered if you had time for a chat.'

'Of course,' said Bertie. 'We could go for a walk on the forest if you like – but not as far as those ponds.'

'I've been wondering if I've upset Bunny,' said Bouncer as they made their way along the banks of the stream and up towards the woods. 'She's announced the next meeting for Thursday, and I'm fairly certain she knew that it was the day I had to be in London.'

'Oh, don't worry about old Bunny,' said Bertie. 'If it's deliberate, she'll soon come round. She's sometimes suspicious of strangers. I don't know why. She was like that when Sheila first came to the village. Now they're good friends.'

They walked on in silence for a while. Suddenly a deer appeared, but was away as soon as it saw them. The rabbits seemed less bothered by these early morning trespassers.

'Sheila told me about your bees and the special way you look after them. I like that idea – respecting the work they do, not taking them for granted.'

Much as Bertie liked the entertaining, high-spirited extrovert who was always in a hurry, he was rather enjoying the company of this quieter, more sub-dued Bouncer. Perhaps all extroverts are a bit shy and fearful at heart, thought Bertie, and they're just trying to hide the fact. Maybe Bouncer was also different this morning, not only because he was clearly hurt by Bunny's apparent rejection, but also because there was no audience to amuse or impress – just the kind and thoughtful companion shuffling along beside him.

Bertie himself always tended to prefer the company of one person at a time. He found that people were more honest in that situation. His friend Peggy could be positively chatty and even quite opinionated when they were alone together on their walks, but was often frightened to open her mouth in a crowd for fear of saying the wrong thing. Bouncer, on the other hand, couldn't keep his mouth shut when surrounded by people.

'I've been thinking recently about *hierarchy* in relation to bees,' said Bertie as they paused beside a clump of pine trees that he was particularly fond of. It was the place he often visited when he felt the need to be alone. A lot of his poems had begun on this spot. 'It's a somewhat provocative word these days,' he added. '"Hierarchy" tends to imply someone bossing about the person further down the ladder than they are, and feeling superior in the process.'

'In my experience it's not how it works in the theatre,' said Bouncer, 'at least not in really creative and successful productions. Everyone listens and learns from each other. The director is more like the conductor of an orchestra than some artistic tyrant.'

'That's interesting,' said Bertie. 'It's how I think nature works, if properly understood; and nature includes us. We may think we're cleverer than, say, fish or birds, but we'd be in big trouble without them; and without trees and ants and flowers. For a start we wouldn't be able to breathe.'

'Wasps, too,' added Bouncer, 'though most people hate them. "What is the point of wasps?" Joey asked me the other day. I'd read recently that they are essential as scavengers, and I told Joey that they are nature's bin men, but able to do their job without blocking up the road every Tuesday morning. I also told him that wasps invented paper long before we did. It's what they make their nests with. Joey then said, "I bet they don't write or draw on it."'

'He's a bright lad, that Joey,' responded Bertie with a smile. 'You can learn a lot from a beehive, too,' he went on. 'Some people think of it as the supreme example of hierarchy, with the queen getting all the attention and the best meals, while the worker bees do just what their name suggests until they drop dead. The drones meanwhile are kicked out once they've played their part and the queen has been fertilised by the dozen or so who can fly the highest as she soars up into the air above the hive.'

'So not all of them make it to that one night stand in the sky!' responded Bouncer, unable to resist making a joke when he felt that Bertie was in danger of becoming too earnest.

Bertie was aware of the tendency he had to sound slightly pompous, but he also recognised the importance of humour and welcomed it. Jokes, like Joey's contributions to the discussion about wasps, were what he missed in his encounters with the Professor. Bouncer's way of referring to that mysterious ritual in which the queen bee is fertilised made him chuckle.

'Our problem', said Bertie, back in serious mode, 'is our very understandable tendency to anthropomorphise, to imagine everything in human terms. But if you see the hive not as some gulag imprisoning its individual members, with the queen in charge, but as one single entity, then you are witnessing cooperation on a magnificent scale.'

'In that sense, maybe our bodies are like beehives,' suggested Bouncer, excited by the way the discussion was going. 'The heart, our lungs, the liver – all have their individual roles so that we can stay alive.'

'You're right,' said Bertie. 'Each organ is absolutely necessary, and therefore no one organ is more important than the other.'

After a pause in which they both felt the need to digest what they had been discussing, and while they watched the sun finally emerge out of the morning mist, Bertie spoke again: 'I've sometimes thought that in the past we spent too much time looking up at the stars and imagining other worlds and gods, and not paying enough attention to what was beneath our feet. Now we do the opposite, but maybe we'll gradually discover that the two belong together.'

'You mean that the universe is one great beehive', laughed Bouncer, 'in which everyone and everything plays an essential part – you, me, wasps and angels? It's a wonderful idea.'

Life in Hartfield – and indeed in the universe at large – seemed unaffected by the profound deliberations of Bertie and Bouncer on what to most people was just an ordinary October morning.

'But nothing is really ordinary' was what Bertie was inclined to believe; and maybe what we think does actually change things, if only slowly.

Meanwhile, on the evening before the next meeting of the Action Group, two separate telephone calls did change things for two of its members. The first was from Bouncer's agent saying that the audition had been cancelled. The second was a call that Bunny made to Sheila.

'I've got to go and see a cousin in the morning. She's just had twins. Her three other children need taking to school, and her shopping to be collected.' Bunny sounded anxious, but she was someone who prided herself on coping, whatever the situation. 'I'll be back by twelve, Sheila, but just in case I only arrive at the last minute, would you please open up the house and let everyone in – the key's in its usual place – and make some coffee?'

Bertie was surprised to see Bouncer heading towards Bunny's house just before midday on the following morning.

Bouncer told him about the phone call from his agent, and Bertie smiled to himself at the thought of Bunny's reaction. Perhaps fate had intervened and the rift would be healed – or so he hoped.

At ten past twelve, with still no sign of Bunny, they decided to start the meeting without her. At that moment the telephone rang and Sheila answered it.

'Fine, fine,' she said. 'Don't worry. We'll start without you, and Peggy will take some notes. By the way, Bouncer's audition was cancelled, so we're pleased he could join us.'

Bertie tried to imagine what Bunny was now thinking and the expression on her face. He exchanged a knowing look with Bouncer, who was still somewhat subdued and secretly worried about Bunny's hostility.

'Pretend you're in a play,' Bouncer said to himself. 'Eventually the curtain will come down, everyone will clap, and you can go home.'

Sheila told them that Bunny's car had broken down earlier that morning, but she was now on her way. The meeting was then officially opened by the Treasurer in lieu of the Chairperson.

The result of the first whorl hunt – or rather the lack of a result – was reported to the Professor, discussed briefly and noted down by Peggy. She then told the meeting that she'd returned to another of the ponds, but without success.

Bertie confirmed that he'd written to two local newspapers and had put notices in several shop windows encouraging people to write to their MP. He also proposed another whorl hunt for Sunday, starting from his house at 2.30 p.m.

The Professor told them that he'd been gathering support on the Internet and that his old college, which owned land and property in Sussex, had promised to use its influence to sway opinion against the bypass.

Sheila then said that she, too, had been out on the forest again, with Joey, but that the snails had obviously heard them coming and hidden themselves. 'Tell them we're trying to help them,' Joey had called out, but obviously not loud enough for them to hear. She also told them that she'd got over one hundred 'likes' on the Facebook page.

The Major still couldn't quite grasp what Facebook was all about, and was clearly not amused by Sheila's joke about Joey and the non-existent snails. Her contribution to the meeting merely confirmed his growing sense that a two-millimetre-long snail – or even a colony of them – was unlikely to win a battle with twelve miles of gravel and tarmac.

At this point in the discussion Bunny finally appeared.

'Glad you could make it,' she mumbled as she passed Bouncer on the way to the empty chair beside Sheila. But both he and Bertie knew that the remark was made more from guilt than from pleasure.

'We've got nothing dramatic to report,' said the Treasurer, 'so why don't you tell us your news.'

'Firstly my apologies for being so late,' said the breathless Chairperson.

How humiliated she must feel, thought Bouncer, but he was determined not to bear a grudge and hoped in time to make friends with her. In his experience most people have a chink somewhere in their armour, and it's often in what may be a very tender place that they can truly meet one another.

'Well, my news is this,' said Bunny, relieved to no longer be feeling quite so anxious, or stupid. 'A contact I've made in the regional office of Highways England told me – very unofficially – that a huge new motorway from the M25 to the south coast between Brighton and Dover is being seriously considered. It would alleviate bottlenecks in places like East Grinstead, and most important of all would make the Hartfield Bypass totally unnecessary.'

'So do we stop worrying?' asked the Professor.

'That's my question, too,' said Sheila.

'No, I don't think so,' was Bunny's immediate response. 'At this stage we can't be certain of this new motorway scheme, and it might take years. Meanwhile the danger is that local considerations – commercial considerations – will push for our bypass to go ahead.'

'Then why is it such important news?' asked the Major, oblivious of the fact that his question implied criticism of Bunny's attention-grabbing message that they'd all received earlier in the week.

'I think Bunny's news is encouraging and therefore important,' volunteered Bouncer. 'Important in that, even if we don't find any whorl snails, we can at least try to delay any decision about the Hartfield bypass long enough for the new motorway to save the day.'

Bouncer said this not only in order to come to Bunny's rescue, but because it was truly what he felt. Bertie added his agreement, and so did the increasingly emboldened Peggy.

As the meeting broke up, Bunny took Bouncer's arm, grateful for his support, and ashamed of her silly prejudices. She asked him what had happened about the audition.

'That's show business!' he said with a big smile.

'Maybe you'd be interested in helping me put on a village pantomime,' she found herself saying. 'We did one a few years ago, but the two stars have since left the village.'

'Why not!' said a relieved Bouncer. 'We could call it *Snow White and the Seven Whorls*.'

CHAPTER SEVEN

In which Peggy starts to feel braver,
and the Major plays soldiers with Joey.

———— ◆ ————

Any sense that the Action Group could relax their efforts was very soon dispelled. The following morning, on her way out of the village to visit one of her nieces, Bunny noticed a rather smart car parked in a lay-by adjoining the forest. Something told her that the vehicle didn't belong either to a local person or to the usual type of visitor to the forest. Having ten minutes or so to spare, she decided to investigate, but discreetly and at a distance.

Indeed the two people she eventually spotted on the brow of a hill were neither walking their dogs nor attired to enjoy the cold and windy forest; in fact one of them was dressed in a suit and was even wearing a tie. Clearly, some sort of survey was going on, as one of the men had a gadget on a tripod – perhaps it was a camera – and the other was on his phone.

Surely such goings-on were premature, thought Bunny. No agreement had been reached about the bypass, and nor would it be for some months – possibly even a year or so. But maybe the Major was right and the whole project was earmarked to go ahead, irrespective of the protests and objections. It was a worried one of those protesters who returned to her car and to her duties for the day.

On the afternoon following the eventful meeting at Bunny's house, Bertie and Peggy were out on the forest enjoying the late autumn sunshine. Evidence of the first frost still lingered in places, but the landscape seemed to be as alive as ever, as were the mistle thrushes, in search of their autumn treat of rowan berries.

The next hunt for whorls was planned for Sunday, but that didn't stop the two friends from pausing from time to time when they came across some likely-looking boggy patch of ground.

'Do you believe in providence, Peggy?' Bertie was in another of his thoughtful moods. The goings-on in the Action Group had stirred up a lot of old questions.

'Not sure what it is,' was Peggy's honest response. 'Do you mean fate?'

'Not exactly. It certainly implies that things are not entirely in our hands. What I do sense is that providence can only intervene if we take the first step, even if it's the wrong one.'

'You mean we can't just sit at home and wait for the phone to ring?' said Peggy. 'We have to be brave and take initiative?'

'That's it, Peggy. Exactly! Put on our hat and coat and go out to fight the dragons. They do still exist, but in clever disguise. Activists are the modern knights.'

'Would you call us activists?' she asked.

'Certainly! Anyone who gets off their backside and doesn't just complain is in my mind an activist. Maybe even writing poetry can sometimes qualify!' Bertie said that with a smile.

Peggy was suddenly quite chuffed to think of herself as a knight, albeit a rather small one.

A sudden urge to sneeze then brought her down to earth. Her first cold of the winter? But knights don't get colds, at least not in the legends she remembered from childhood. Was she really getting braver? Perhaps laughing at herself was a first step. She knew very well the sorts of things that made her anxious, all of which became very much worse when she was on her own.

The recent meetings had certainly awakened in Peggy a feeling that things can and indeed do change if we're bold enough to question our routine and above all our patterns of thought. She was even starting to feel inclined to talk to someone about her early life, a subject she had deliberately buried for years. Bertie would be the obvious person, but in a strange way she felt that Bouncer, the loud and large Bouncer, the person who had already rocked Bunny's boat, might be the person in whom she could confide about why she always felt so timid, why she had never married and why she sensed danger round every corner. Years ago she had bought a small car, but she only kept it a couple of years. She remembered how Bertie had teased her when she said that she didn't like to drive at night in case the car broke down on some remote lane.

'What happens if it doesn't?' he had said.

Perhaps she and Bertie knew each other too well, she thought, and their image of one another had inevitably become somewhat fixed, though warmly so. Maybe this strange man Bouncer, whom she sensed was a lot more sensitive than his extrovert behaviour conveyed, would come fresh to the mystery that was Peggy.

On that same afternoon, and blissfully unaware of what was going on in Peggy's mind, Bouncer found himself enjoying a cup of tea and a slice of coffee cake with his very new friend, Bunny. How strange, he thought, that what we do and feel on one day can seem so totally inappropriate on the next.

The reason for the invitation was to discuss the idea of a village pantomime, but Bouncer knew – and Bunny also knew – that what lay behind the invitation was her feeling of shame at letting her silly prejudices upset another person. Fortunately, this didn't have to be discussed, thanks to Bouncer's enthusiastic response to the pantomime idea.

'The problem', Bunny was saying, 'is that it's rather late in the year to produce something in time for Christmas. Also people are so busy in December, and the schools don't break up until the twentieth. It's nice to involve some children.'

'What about something in February?' suggested Bouncer. 'It's a dull month that needs cheering up.'

'Yes, but a Christmas pantomime would seem rather out of date by then, don't you think?'

Bouncer then had a brilliant idea – or so it seemed at the time.

'What about a Valentine's Day celebration on February 14th? It could have all the silly ingredients of a pantomime – men dressed up as women, a villain and a hero, references to dodgy goings-on in the village – and above all it would be fun.'

'Great!' said Bunny, though she did wonder for a moment what Bouncer was implying by 'dodgy goings-on in the village'.

By now Bouncer's theatrical imagination was whirring. A love story on Valentine's Day!

'The Major – or perhaps the Professor – could be Prince Charming; and Princess Peggy could be woken from her hundred years of sleep by a peck on the cheek.'

'You'd never get the Major to act on a stage, nor the Professor,' said Bunny as she cut Bouncer another slice of cake.

'All right, you could be Prince Charming!' he said with a chuckle. 'We could call it *Heartaches in Hartfield*.'

In her response Bunny was careful not to reveal her slight regret at what she had set in motion. 'Let's live with the idea for a day or so,' she said with a smile.

Meanwhile what Bertie called providence was already hovering in the wings, excited at the idea of being able to help with the theatrical challenge that might lie ahead.

At the other end of the village two other encounters took place that day, both with significant implications for those involved. The Professor had an appointment with his doctor to hear about the results of some recent tests. It was worrying news. He'd read from time to time in the newspaper about certain medical problems that can affect older men, but like most people his reaction had always been 'Thank God it's not me'. Now all that had suddenly changed. It was his turn to be faced with the reality of his own mortality.

Meanwhile, that afternoon, Sheila had called round to see the Major, who was having 'a spot of bother with the electrics'. She already had a reputation for being one of the most practical people in the village, always ready to help in an emergency, and unfazed by fuse boxes, wasp nests and even blocked drains. When she was growing up in the outback of Australia there hadn't been what Bunny still called 'a little man' to phone when the slightest problem arose.

Sheila had taken Joey with her, making him promise that he'd play quietly and not disturb the Major – or 'the wombat', as she secretly still thought of him. In fact quite another situation developed, which turned out to be as surprising to Sheila – and later to other people in the village – as it was to the Major.

Joey had taken with him a box containing his precious collection of toy soldiers, plus three army trucks, a field gun and two tanks. They'd been a present from the Australian night watchman for his fifth birthday; not what Sheila would have chosen, but on the other hand, she thought, it was probably better to play at that sort of game aged five than at twenty-five.

Joey had no idea that the old man in the armchair reading his *Daily Telegraph* had once been an actual soldier; and because the Major never talked about war, or about anything else to do with his life, most of the village also never thought of him in those terms, despite the attachment to his rank by which they knew him.

However, the sight of this battle in miniature unfolding on the carpet at his feet was to have an extraordinary effect on the old warrior, and eventually even brought a twinkle to his eye, so Sheila told Bunny the following day.

At first the Major had just glanced at Joey from time to time out of the corner of his eye, but was still busy reading his newspaper. However, the sight of the toy soldiers gradually proved irresistible, and he started to suggest some tactics as if to his young subaltern. Joey liked the ideas, repositioned his troops and then asked the Major if he'd ever seen a real tank.

That was it; the floodgates then opened! For the next ten minutes the saga of the Korean War and the exploits of a young lieutenant in a Centurion tank were related to a bewildered five-year-old who nonetheless was gripped by the drama and excitement of it all and entranced by this spluttering old man beside him who had fought in a real tank.

From her precarious position on top of a ladder by the back door, Sheila heard the Major's voice rattling on, occasionally interrupted by squeals of laughter and delight from Joey, and wondered what on earth they were talking about. Having never heard the Major utter more than a few words, and those were usually grumpy ones, she wondered what magic it was that had created so animated a bond between two such very different people.

When, over the next few days, news gradually reached Bertie about the various happenings on that autumn Friday, he found himself wondering if all those conversations, all those very different voices – his and Peggy's, Bunny with Bouncer, the Major and Joey, the Professor with his doctor – were also heard by and of interest to what he sometimes thought of as 'our invisible friends'.

His mother had often spoken about angels in a very matter-of-fact way, and when he was a child they were as real to him as people, animals and the huge beech tree that grew at the bottom of their garden.

Bertie was hesitant to use the word 'God', not because he didn't believe in something infinitely wiser than we are, but rather because for him the word had so many unhelpful connotations. He'd once heard someone refer to this mysterious being as the 'Management'. It wasn't said as a joke, and Bertie felt that the word expressed very well what is actually impossible for us to understand or imagine, and yet did so with a light but respectful touch.

The Management certainly had its hands full with all the goings-on in this little English village, where relationships were shifting fast and where a variety of knights, without either spears or swords, were preparing to do battle with a dragon whose size they could hardly imagine.

Chapter Eight

*In which the Professor shares his bad news,
and nobody finds a whorl.*

———— ·◆·◆· ————

Sunday's hunt for whorls was a cheerful occasion, not least because the Major didn't grumble and instead spent a lot of his time answering an endless stream of questions from Joey, not all of them about warfare.

'Why have you got hair under your nose?'

'Haven't you ever seen a moustache, young man?' responded the old soldier.

'Only on Father Christmas, but I've never really *seen* him.'

The next question – 'Do worms have mouths?' – was a rather harder one to answer, particularly because the subject of biology hadn't featured much in the Major's life, either at school or in the army.

Sheila was delighted by Joey's friendship with the Major. He'd needed a man in his life, and now he had two. Bouncer was an exciting and playful friend – at times almost like a child himself – who read Joey stories and, best of all, would sometimes make them up. The Major, on the other hand, was held in awe, and Joey was already asking when he could go to his house again to play soldiers.

On the walk, Peggy chatted with Bouncer and was feeling less and less intimidated by him, even though he was a real actor who had probably had his name up in lights in the West End. Nevertheless she was certainly not ready to talk with him about what she recognised as her baggage and her increasing need to unload it; and not even to share with him the fact that she herself had once known an actor.

For his part Bouncer was already beginning to sense that there was more to Peggy than first appeared. In fact, in his experience, there was more to most people if you gave them time to show it; and more important than time was for them to feel that you were genuinely interested.

Trailing along behind were Sheila and Bertie, deep in conversation with Bunny about the latest news on the bypass situation. She told them about the scene she had witnessed and the man with a tripod and wearing a tie. This information, plus the possibility of a new motorway – a project that might solve all their problems – meant that the whorls were hardly given a thought.

It was Bouncer who finally reminded them all of why they were on the forest, and for half an hour or so everyone stopped talking – even Joey – and spread out along the banks of the stream in search of what could be a much more immediate and simple answer to their prayers.

Only the Professor was missing from this latest expedition. He'd again excused himself, but no one yet knew the reason. He'd also just cancelled his forthcoming talk to the History Society, which rather alarmed Bertie. His friend's devotion to those monthly meetings was legendary.

The Professor was, of course, in shock; and as he absent-mindedly wound up the clock on his mantelpiece for the second time this week, he was suddenly very aware that the mechanism that keeps us human beings ticking is far more complicated than even the most intricate of machines. And in that same moment he realised, too, why 'mechanism' was such an inappropriate word to use when referring to something as mysterious and complex as the human body.

The next morning, Bertie decided to visit the Professor in case he was still un-well. He even took along a jar of his honey, knowing that it might help to stave off autumn sniffles.

It was, of course, no sniffle that the Professor was now eager to dis-cuss with someone. What he suddenly needed was comfort, help and advice. The friend now on his way was, of course, the perfect person. Bertie was kind, thoughtful and even – dare the Professor admit it – actually quite wise, despite his irritating block about science and technology.

In fact Bertie felt that he had no real problem with science. He recog-nised that it was, after all, one important example of humanity's basic spirit of enquiry; a curiosity that had existed long before the word 'science' was ever invented. Nor did he have a problem with that aspect of our enquiry which manifests as technology, starting – he was once reminded – with the wheel and the plough. It was computers that he couldn't quite cope with, though at a very basic level he was grateful to be able to send and receive emails and to access information so easily and quickly. That was how he learnt about the many small and idealistic initiatives taking place all over the world, undertaken particularly by younger people, but hardly ever reported in the newspapers. Deeds, rather than just words, were what gave him hope.

Bertie was grateful, too, for the science that had made possible his cen-tral heating and his electric kettle. He tried not to take for granted even a fa-miliar device like the telephone. For him it was all a question of balance and, above all, of avoiding the danger not just of becoming slaves to our machines, but of becoming machine-like in the process. After a recent, and particularly frustrating and heartless telephone conversation with his electricity supplier, he had said to Peggy that he felt it was our very humanity that was at stake.

'What do you mean?' Peggy had asked him as they sat at her kitchen table after their last walk and their talk about modern-day knights.

'Well, these modern gadgets are so clever and so seductive, allowing us to organise and fill up our lives so that not a moment is wasted, but ...'

Bertie had paused, aware he might be seen once again as sticking his head in the sand, even by Peggy.

'Go on,' she then said. 'You're not as alone as you think, dear Bertie. Look how often the word "stress" crops up these days. Technology allows us to do so much, so easily, but the danger is we do nothing properly, nothing in depth. We can be in touch with so many people, and yet not truly in touch with anyone.'

'That's exactly it,' Bertie said.

Yet again he'd experienced the wisdom that was so often concealed behind his friend's timidity; a wisdom that he suspected was far more prevalent in the world at large than appears at first glance. The survival of our humanity might be at stake, but human beings still had some life in them and were not going to lie down easily; and certainly not as long as they could still laugh and make jokes, particularly about themselves.

However, from time to time his fear that we might lose this battle would bring on his fits of depression. He tried to keep them to himself: no point in dragging other people down with him. Perhaps he was too proud to reveal his weaknesses? But he also recognised that, despite these concerns, it was his contact with other people that not only took his mind off his own worries – including his occasional loneliness – but also nurtured his essential optimism. Above all, it was the little acts of kindness that he constantly witnessed amid the rush and pressures of daily life that gave him hope.

'Good to see you, Bertie' – a polite greeting from the Professor, but also words that on this occasion came truly from the heart.

'We missed you yesterday – but no whorls to report!'

When the two of them had settled down by the fire – the Professor enjoyed his home comforts – Bertie asked him whether his cold was better.

'Oh that! No problem. But a bit of bad news from my doctor.'

'What's the matter? Not that rheumatism back again?'

'No, it's what I believe they call "the old man's disease".'

'You mean the prostate? Is it serious?'

'I'm afraid so – cancer – and too advanced to operate. The scan showed that it had started to spread.'

'Oh, Prof, I am sorry,' said Bertie. 'I had no idea you …'

'… had to pee three or four times in the night! Why should you?' said his friend with something bordering on a smile.

There was a pause while the Professor put a couple of logs on the fire.

'Cup of coffee?'

'No thanks; unless you want one.'

Bertie would like to have asked for a biscuit, but in the circumstances it felt inappropriate. Instead he respected the moment of silence that his friend seemed to want.

'I suppose until recently I just took my health for granted,' the Professor then continued. 'We all do, I suppose, until something starts to hurt or doesn't work properly.'

'What does the doctor recommend?'

'Something called hormones. Don't fancy it at all. And maybe chemo-therapy.'

'What about talking to Sheila?'

'Why Sheila? She's not a doctor.'

'No, but she takes quite an interest in health, especially in alternative – or rather what's called complementary medicine.'

'Not touching that stuff, old fellow. You know my opinion about all these unproven remedies. I suppose she's into homeopathy and that sort of thing.'

Bertie was not surprised by the Professor's response. Perhaps he should hold back on such suggestions for a while. Nevertheless he still thought it worth trying to involve Sheila at some point. Perhaps a crisis – and this certainly was one – would gradually soften the Professor's attitude.

'Maybe I could bring her to see you sometime, Prof. There's no hurry. I could stick around if you like, so you can always let off steam at me if you need to!'

'I'll think about it; but meanwhile no word to anyone else. I'm aware that I need to talk, but I'm not quite sure what it is that I want to say. When I do, I imagine the right person will appear.'

After another pause came the question that had obviously been on the Professor's mind ever since the visit to his doctor on Friday.

'Do you think much about death, Bertie?'

'Quite often, actually,' he replied, 'and, when I do, I always find it hard to imagine that anyone I know will completely disappear.'

'We live on in other people's memories; that I recognise,' said his friend. 'But our actual individual existence is clearly over.'

'Our physical existence, yes. But a lot of what we are – in some ways the most important parts – like our thoughts and feelings, and the bonds we feel with one another – are not really physical. You certainly can't put those things under a microscope. You can't weigh joy and sorrow.'

'But they need a physical body to manifest, my dear Bertie. No thoughts without a brain.'

Bertie wasn't quite out of his depth, but it was close. How do you put into words something that is deeply felt but is so difficult to express in everyday language? Two plus two always makes four, thought Bertie; likewise we put food in our mouths and not up our noses; we don't try to walk on water. But …

'I'm not so sure about this idea that thoughts are generated in the brain,' he volunteered bravely.

'Stick in there,' Bertie said to himself. Maybe deep down the Professor is longing to be challenged – even contradicted – and, faced with the possibility of his own death, he's probably engaged in much more than an academic argument about mortality. Perhaps his religion and his science – his head and his heart – are no longer quite so happy in their separate compartments.

'What if the brain is more like a receiver of thoughts, rather than their source – rather like a television set?' Bertie continued. 'If you open up the set, you won't find any programmes inside it. However, you've clearly got problems if the set is damaged. The programmes are still there, but you can't access them. Likewise someone with brain damage can't think so well, or maybe at all, but that doesn't prove that their thoughts originated in the brain.'

All this was too much for Bertie's learned friend. Just because he was ill, and maybe even dying, he wasn't suddenly going to start looking at life in a totally new and alien way. However, what he did need, he realised, and needed more than ever, was sympathetic company, whatever nonsense that company might believe in. A visit from someone like Sheila was therefore already starting to feel quite welcome, though maybe without that child of hers. Never having had children himself, he found such obsessive devotion quite incomprehensible and rather irritating.

The Professor, like Joey, was an only child, but remembered his parents as being rather remote. Boarding school from an early age had reinforced the feeling that he was essentially on his own. His university colleagues had been colleagues but not close friends. Instead he felt blessed to have discovered books from an early age and to have been given the chance to pursue an academic career, largely protected from the rough and tumble that most people have to face.

But now suddenly he was confronted *by* that rough and tumble and by the realisation that at the end of the day we're all in the same boat. In the coming days and weeks, the thought that maybe this could be a very healing experience slowly started to occur to this distinguished but somewhat troubled citizen of Hartfield.

CHAPTER NINE

In which Sheila and Bouncer have a good gossip,
while Bertie and Bunny discuss the meaning of life.

———————— • • ————————

Sheila and Bouncer, having finished breakfast and in no hurry to get on with the day, were in the mood for a chat. There were no distractions from Joey, who had built a tank from the sofa cushions and was busy in a life-or-death battle with a platoon of North Korean soldiers who were holed up behind one of the armchairs.

'What's Bertie's story?' asked Bouncer, eager to know more about this colourful band of people with whom he had so quickly become involved.

'Nobody really knows. He doesn't ever talk about his past. He just is, and maybe that's how he's always been. In another age I could imagine him being some sort of hermit – but a very friendly one! I've heard the Professor refer to him as "alternative", which is his polite way of saying that our friend has weird ideas.'

'More that his ideas that don't fit in with scientific orthodoxy, I suspect,' said Bouncer.

'You're probably right. Anyway, he's one of those rare people who seems to be totally at peace with himself, is friends with everyone and doesn't want or need complicated attachments; though I sometimes wonder what goes on when he's on his own and whether the warmth and concern he shows for others comes at a certain cost. And he can be a bit preachy at times.'

'I can imagine him once being a schoolteacher,' said Bouncer, 'though he could just as well have been a postman or a librarian. What do you make of his poetry?'

'I'm no judge. Don't forget I'm from the outback of Australia! There a spade is a bloody spade. Who cares what the actual word rhymes with!'

'Come on, Sheila! You're not such a philistine as all that. What about all those strange medicines you're interested in and dish out to Joey? Or perhaps you're an Aboriginal Australian at heart!'

'They know a thing or two, those guys. We've been so busy forgetting, in our endless pursuit of knowledge – some of it helpful, I grant you – but it's time we did some remembering.'

'You're sounding like old Bertie,' said Bouncer. 'I had an interesting chat with him the other day. He was talking about his bees and about hierarchy. He even brought up the subject of God. You know that he has this strong feeling that everything is interconnected. I liked what he said.'

'He's a wise fellow, I agree. When I first came to the village I was puzzled for a while by this friendship he has with Peggy. But I reckon there's more to her than meets the eye.'

'I agree. Maybe that's what Bertie sees, or at least senses. She's become quite chatty with me recently.'

'And Bunny?' Bouncer then asked. '*There's* a bundle of contradictions if ever there was one!'

'She was prickly with me at first; with you, too, I suspect. But there's a lot of heart behind all that busyness. It's a side of the English that I'm still trying to get used to. Polite, usually kind, but – my God – some of them aren't half buttoned up! … What about you, Bouncer? You don't seem to be buttoned up. Why are you on your own?'

'Perhaps being gay has something to do with it, though some of the happiest couples I know are gay. Anyway, to answer your question, I've never wanted to shack up with anyone. Another of life's loners, I suppose – but quite a happy one.'

Sheila was touched by Bouncer's honesty and gave him a hug.

'And you, Sheila? Where is Joey's dad?'

'Far away, and not just physically. No regrets … though a partner would be nice. Maybe stop me fussing over Joey so much. Bunny keeps saying I should have more children, but doesn't seem bothered about who the father would be!'

They paused to glance at the battle still underway on the sitting-room floor. The enemy was clearly on its last legs.

'I'm thinking of training as a psychotherapist,' Sheila then volunteered. 'Plenty of experience of wounds. Perhaps I could help to heal other people's.'

There was no time to describe what those wounds were. The phone was ringing, Joey wanted a drink, and anyway, thought Sheila, perhaps they had said enough for the time being.

After the turmoil of the last few days – news of a possible new motorway, the embarrassing outcome of her plot to exclude Bouncer from the Action Group, and then the unexpected bond developing with her victim – Bunny felt in need of a walk on the forest; it was the nearest she ever got to relaxing. Maybe Bertie would join her, preferably without Peggy trotting along beside them. They could keep an eye out for whorls at the same time, though Bunny was fast giving up hope on that somewhat crazy idea.

Hat and new wax coat, sensible shoes, and she was off to Church Lane.

As she peeped through his window, she could see Bertie snoozing in his arm-chair. It was nearly three o'clock; high time to wake him up, she thought.

Ten minutes later they were making their way towards one of her fa-vourite spots on the forest. A strong wind was blowing away the few remaining leaves, but out in the open the clumps of gorse were as radiant as ever. Soon, she thought, the trees would look as Bertie had described them in one of his poems – like 'skeletons of summer'. It was one of the few phrases she remembered from what he had written over the years.

Bertie himself wasn't feeling either chatty or particularly aware of their surroundings; or indeed of his appearance. One trouser leg was tucked into the corresponding boot; the other flapped about in the wind. He couldn't stop thinking about the Professor and their conversation about death. But because he'd promised not to tell anyone about what the doctor had said – not even Bunny or Peggy – he felt even more haunted by the news. He was also aware of how inadequate his own response had been to the crisis. Why should what he felt about a subject as mysterious as death be of any help to another person, par-ticularly to someone in such shock? Like all of us, he told himself, the Professor has finally to find what makes sense to *him*; and that might be anything out of a whole range of options, with faith and trust at one end, to outright rejection of any notion of meaning and immortality at the other.

'Essentially we're all on our own,' was Bertie's thought at that moment – and above all when facing what the Professor was now facing. And perhaps most people's fear of death is because we don't really understand life. Meanwhile he hoped that the concern and affection that would soon surround the Prof would at least be of some comfort to him.

All these different thoughts and ideas were spinning around in Bertie's head as he stumped along beside the formidable Bunny. She, on the other hand, was preoccupied with concerns about a possible Valentine's Day entertainment instead of a pantomime. She recognised her attachment to tradition – it helped to make life feel safe – but she also sensed that to do things differently and above all to think differently was a challenge she had tended to avoid. Bouncer, whose presence and manner had initially irritated her, was now perhaps – in some strange way – a catalyst of change, or at least a shift in how she went about her daily life.

'What do you make of Bouncer?' she asked Bertie as they paused to catch their breath on the brow of a hill. Overhead a flock of crows were swoop-ing on a sparrowhawk. No eggs to protect at this time of year, so was it just habit?

'Is that how you felt about him?' asked Bertie with a smile as he pointed to the battle going on above them.

'It wasn't that bad – but I suppose so,' was Bunny's honest response. 'It was the same when Sheila first turned up in the village. What is it, Bertie, that makes us reject strangers and resist change?'

'Perhaps it's insecurity. I don't know. Routine and habit are very basic instincts in all of us. For animals such things determine their whole life. But I sometimes feel that we human beings have an extra task, to create what has never existed before.'

'Like what?' asked Bunny.

Bertie hesitated. He'd long been wary of loading onto others what constantly occupied him in the silence of his own company – thoughts that seemed not to deeply interest most other people. Yet Bunny had asked a question, so why not have a go at answering it?

'Well, take the example of bees,' he said. 'They create honey; they do it every year, and in the process the whole of nature – of which we are a part – benefits. But they are extremely unlikely to produce marmalade one year!'

Bunny smiled at the idea of Bertie scooping out marmalade from one of his hives.

'Whereas our creativity', he went on, 'is open-ended; we're not specialists like everything else in nature, but we have the potential to create something new.'

'And what is that, Bertie?'

Now he was getting into really deep water. Should he just stop and admit defeat? Utter the familiar phrase, 'We can't know'? Bunny still seemed to be listening, still seemed to be interested. Yet how could he describe the creativity he had in mind?

'These are questions that I ask myself almost every day, Bunny. What am I here for? What are we all here for? Is there meaning in it all, or is it one great game of chance? There was a German philosopher – I forget his name – who once asked the most challenging question of all: "Why is there something, rather than nothing?"'

There was a pause as a gust of wind caused both of them to stumble. Ahead of them a rabbit shot into the heather.

'You're losing me, Bertie. I'll need to take a breather before I ask you any more questions!'

As they set off back towards home, the familiar, energetic Bunny was back in the saddle. Bertie, too, was happy that the business of daily life – including his impending afternoon tea – was no longer being put on hold in the pursuit of what could so easily become no more than words. Nevertheless he had a strong hunch that involvement with that daily life, if it were lived with heart and eyes open, could help to ensure that conversations like the one he had just started with Bunny need not become mere abstraction. In fact, he felt that daily life, however mundane it might appear, was what really mattered; it's how people learn and grow. They might not all read the books he read, or ask the questions he asked, but he believed that everyone – whether conscious of it or not – was on a journey, a meaningful journey, and that at heart they were doing their best.

'Let's come down to earth,' Bunny said as they descended the windswept hill. It was as though she had picked up the same thought, but in her own way.

'What about Bouncer's crazy idea for celebrating St Valentine's Day?' she asked him. 'Are you up for playing Prince Charming in front of the whole village, Bertie?'

The two friends spent the rest of the walk chatting about the here and now, but Bertie was careful to steer way from the subject of the Professor. He hoped that the illness would not have to be kept a secret for long and that every-one could join together to help their friend through whatever lay ahead.

'Any plans for another meeting of the Action Group?' Bertie asked as they approached the village.

'No point until we have some more news – or until someone turns up with a real, live whorl! Plans for a Public Consultation are underway; and there's no news yet from any of Christopher's contacts in Whitehall. I imagine all sorts of conversations and plotting are going on at another level.'

Before they parted, a more subdued Bunny said quietly to Bertie, 'Why have we never had this sort of talk before?'

'You mean the one we had up on the forest?'

'Yes; and about things that really matter.'

Bertie paused. Perhaps he had said enough, and yet he felt that the conversation wasn't quite over and that Bunny's question about the potential of human beings still needed answering.

'I think that moments like this happen at the right time, like much else that we meet in life. Perhaps we need to have greater trust in what's going on behind the scenes, as it were – and in a wisdom we can barely grasp.'

'Go on.'

'Well, I have a hunch that the answer to the question about humanity creating what's quite new has something to do with love – and not just the love we have instinctively for family and for like-minded friends.'

Bunny immediately thought of the two colleagues at the Citizens Advice Bureau who irritated her intensely. Her immediate reaction to Bertie's sermon was that loving them might take several lifetimes. He, meanwhile, was hoping very much that what he was saying *didn't* sound like a sermon. But he also felt that something else still needed saying.

'Someone once said – I think it was Gandhi – that one day, perhaps far into the future, it will be impossible for us to feel at peace while another person suffers. In other words we'll slowly start to experience each other's pain and sorrow as if it were our own.'

'There's a beautiful sentence that comes up in church sometimes about "the love that surpasses all understanding",' responded Bunny. 'But I've always imagined that that is what God and his angels are supposed to feel: unconditional love. If that's so, why do you use the word "new"?'

'Well, maybe God has no choice, whereas we human beings are capable of quite the opposite of love. We therefore *have* a choice ... and if we do gradually start to care about the other person – every person – as much as we care about ourselves, a new sort of love will come into being; a love that is arrived at without compulsion, but in freedom. Very idealistic, I know, but I believe we're on our way; a shift *is* taking place.'

Then came another pause. Bertie gazed into the distance.

'But that shift takes time,' he then added. 'Sometimes a very long time.'

Bertie now seemed to be talking quietly to himself and to the forest as much as he was talking to Bunny. For a brief moment she too had the feeling that the trees and the heather, the birds and the insects were listening. Perhaps that's what Bertie had meant by humanity's creativity. It was almost as though nature, and not just God, was waiting for human beings to take the next step, whatever that was.

As if reading her thoughts, Bertie spoke again: 'And maybe that shift is what we call evolution.'

Slowly a smile came over his face. 'I've remembered a joke.'

Bertie was back on earth.

'"The Stone Age didn't come to an end because we ran out of stones!"'

CHAPTER TEN

In which the Professor's routine is interrupted,
and Peggy unburdens herself to Bouncer.

For the last day or so the Professor hadn't felt much like working on the book he was writing about irrigation in medieval Europe. Normally he stuck to a very strict routine: writing in the morning, starting no later than nine o'clock; a light lunch at one was followed by a short nap, and then work again until six. He enjoyed a glass of sherry before supper, and the rest of the evening he spent reading. He didn't much care for television, but quite often listened to what he still called the wireless. Only church on Sundays interrupted his weekly routine, but it was the familiarity of the ritual and the music rather than the Christian doctrine that appealed to him.

Meals were initially a problem after his retirement, since he had never had to cook in his life. Nowadays he relied on ready-made meals, or anything else that just needed heating up. Rice pudding from a tin, with homemade jam from the WI, was his favourite pudding; and sometimes Bunny would bring him one of her apple crumbles. He kept a good cellar, having been in charge of the wine at his college for many years. As a young man he had often holidayed in southwest France, and he knew many of the vineyards around Bordeaux.

Although he lived on his own, the Professor hadn't felt lonely since his retirement. In some ways he felt that living in the village was much like his life in college: familiar faces, people to talk to if you felt inclined, but everyone minding their own business – or so he thought!

Now things suddenly seemed very different. It wasn't just the prospect of death that troubled him – death was unimaginable, so he'd never given it much thought – but rather the impending disruption to his routine. If he didn't feel inclined to work, what else would he do?

This morning at breakfast he treated himself to a boiled egg plus a bowl of porridge; usually it was one or the other. He then decided to phone Bertie and follow up the suggestion of a visit from Sheila. They'd only ever exchanged a few words, but he had sensed that she was a breath of fresh air in the village, despite her rather brash manner; 'a free spirit' was the phrase that came to mind.

Thus the idea of talking to a relative stranger suddenly seemed quite attractive; and perhaps, as Bertie had suggested, she might have some helpful advice about his problem, as long as it didn't involve doing yoga and eating raw vegetables.

On that same day that the Professor was contemplating the unknown, Peggy and Bouncer found themselves on the path leading to the forest at exactly the same time. Was it just chance? If, like Bertie, you don't believe in such a thing as chance, then something else was at work, or so Peggy later thought.

'How come you're called Bouncer?' she asked him as they crossed the little bridge over the stream.

'Well, apparently as a small boy I used to love bouncing on the beds in the morning as they were being made. I do remember the bouncing, and the songs my mother used to sing. I think my bounces were in time to the songs.'

'What sort of songs? Do you remember them?'

'Well, I remember one about "no more monkeys jumping on the bed"; and then there was "Old Macdonald". According to my mother's version, alongside his duck and his pig and his cow the farmer had a lion and a tiger and even a crocodile!'

Peggy smiled at the thought of the huge man walking beside her as a little boy playing games with his mother while she tried to make the beds.

'And your family, Bouncer?'

'Well, my grandfather was a Bengali poet – quite a famous one. He married an English nurse from Bristol. Quite a lot of ruffled feathers at the time – on both sides of the world!'

'Have you ever been to India?'

'No, but I'd love to. My grandfather came from Calcutta.' Bouncer smiled; in his mind, and just for a moment, he was almost there. 'And you, Peggy? Nobody seems to know much about you in the village – your past, I mean.'

So here at last was the opportunity to talk about her life and all the things she had deliberately buried for so long. But was she brave enough? And why talk to Bouncer whom she hardly knew? Why talk to anyone?

'Well, I was the youngest of eight children,' she began. 'Small and timid from the start. Sometimes my sisters called me the runt. We lived on a farm, and I would go and hide in one of the barns when they teased me. I remember a friend of my brothers chasing me with a watering can to make me grow.'

Peggy paused. She needed to give Bouncer these facts, but what she really wanted to share was what she had experienced inwardly as she was growing up.

'How come that I was frightened of everything, and other children seemingly not? It's almost as though I was born frightened. What is that, Bouncer?'

'My grandfather would have had no problem answering that question, Peggy. In India they believe in reincarnation: that we come into each new life with baggage from previous lives; baggage that contains both strengths and weaknesses.'

'You mean I was frightened in a previous life?'

'Maybe, though it's probably more complicated than that. It's a mystery, Peggy, and I love mysteries.' Bouncer paused to run his hands over the trunk of a young silver birch tree. 'This tree is a mystery, if you think about it,' he said with a smile. 'We are more complicated mysteries, I suppose, though it does seem obvious to me that our characters – and therefore our destinies – cannot be explained simply by our genes and by the environment in which we grew up. A DNA test will only reveal details of our physical inheritance.'

'What you seem to be saying is that if we were wise enough we could tap into our spiritual DNA,' responded Peggy.

'That's a good way of putting it. You should ask Bertie what he thinks.'

'Maybe I should. Anyway, to go on with the story, this rather lonely and timid child that was me helped on the farm, but was never afraid of the animals.'

'Where was it, the farm?'

'In Devon, just inland from that wild north coast. I then left school at sixteen and went to a secretarial college in Barnstaple. I still felt out of place. The other girls were so confident; to me they were more like young women than girls. I had a boyfriend for a while, but he was almost more timid than I was. We never even kissed.'

'Not like nowadays!' laughed Bouncer. 'I knew almost nothing about sex until my early twenties. But, unlike you, I had a strange sort of confidence that life was on my side. For whatever reason, this optimism seemed to be there as part of my baggage – but there were complicated bits, too.'

'Like what?'

'Another time, perhaps. Let's go on talking about you. What happened next?'

'Well, I went to stay with my godmother in London and got a job as a secretary. By that time I think both my parents were exhausted – exhausted by the farm and by having brought up eight children.'

Peggy paused. It had started to rain, but only the soft kind of rain that hardly makes you wet. Bouncer buttoned up his coat and waited. Peggy dabbed away a tear or two and blew her nose. It was a funny little nose, thought Bouncer, but it suited her.

'Now comes the really tricky bit,' she said. 'I don't know why I'm telling you this, Bouncer. It's the baggage, as you call it, that I carry still – not from a past life, but from thirty years ago.'

'You don't have to tell me, Peggy. Some things need to be kept private.'

'Maybe, but not if they gnaw away and undermine your whole exist-ence. Anyway, here we go. I met an actor at a party – at least he said he was an actor. I was flattered that someone with such a glamorous career seemed to be interested in me. After a couple of months I moved in with him, and soon after that he suggested a holiday in the Caribbean as a celebration. I'd never been abroad, except on a school trip to France.'

'What was his name, this actor? Maybe I know him.'

'There's no point in telling you. I'm sure he wasn't really an actor. Any way, when we flew back from Jamaica my suitcase was searched at Heathrow, and I was taken straight to prison on remand, to Holloway.'

'How dreadful, Peggy. I've heard stories like that before; men using in-nocent girls to smuggle in drugs. What on earth happened next?'

'It was terrible in prison – such sad, angry, vulnerable women; many separated from their children, even from their babies. At the trial my friend ignored me completely. He was sentenced to fifteen years, I think it was; I was acquitted.'

Peggy gazed into the distance, and into a whole series of images and emotions from the past. Bouncer respected the silence she seemed to need. They paused at the brow of a hill, and Peggy blew her nose again. She then looked up at Bouncer with a look of relief and gratitude.

'I then went to look after my godmother who'd moved down here to Hartfield,' she continued. 'I nursed her for almost ten years, and when she died she left me her cottage and just sufficient money to carry on living as I do now. Not really such an interesting story, but it's mine and it's what I live with.'

'Every story is interesting, Peggy. Everyone's story matters, and not just to them. How wonderful that you have a friend like Bertie. Maybe he's the secret jewel smuggled in among that baggage you brought, not into Heathrow, but into life.'

'Do you think that we've known some people before – before this life, I mean?'

'The Hindus would say so.'

'But you, Bouncer. What do you believe?'

'It would make sense. Most people when they die probably feel a sense of unfinished business. And perhaps it's only in life that we have the possibility to put right the hurt and the mess we left behind last time.'

'Though some relationships, just a few, feel like blessings,' said Peg-gy. 'No more quarrels; just love and unconditional support. Life's not all bad, Bouncer. That's what I'm slowly starting to learn; and talking to you has made me feel braver. I'm very grateful.'

By four o'clock it was already starting to get dark, but life in the village continued as usual. Hartfield had its own version of rush hour – school traffic, and a few commuters already starting to make their way home. It was a mild affair compared with gridlocks on the M25 a few miles to the north, but in the eyes of those who favoured a bypass it was ample ammunition. Most people were too busy to bother either way.

Also making their way home were Peggy and Bouncer – she not quite with a spring in her step, but to the discerning eye someone from whom a weight had clearly been lifted.

Bunny, too, was feeling braver, but in her case the change was prompted by having briefly stepped aside from what usually occupied her, and from all that stuff whirring around in her head from morning till night. She'd been inspired by her conversation with Bertie on the forest, particularly by his faith in human potential.

'What is mine?' she had started to wonder. 'It might certainly be helped if I stopped rushing about so much, read some books and maybe took up the piano again'.

She also wanted to ask Bertie what he meant when he'd said that we're frightened of death because we don't understand life. Bunny couldn't get that particular thought out of her mind. Like most people, she had tended not to think about the subject of death that much, but was always deeply saddened when friends or relations passed away; it seemed so final.

But that phrase itself – 'passed away' – didn't help, she thought. True, some people would say 'passed on', but the idea was much the same. From the perspective of those left behind, it was basically a loss and an ending.

As she sat at her desk making a list of things to remember for tomorrow – including to slow down – Bunny didn't yet know to what extent, in the coming weeks, this subject of death was going to dominate her life so dramatically.

Chapter Eleven

*In which Sheila's advice is rejected,
and Bunny sheds a tear.*

———— • ▬ • ————

'I don't want people bringing me grapes and books about the afterlife,' was the Professor's initial response to his visitors' offer of help.

The Professor is in good form, thought Bertie, considering the crisis he is facing. Perhaps it's because of Sheila's presence that he is putting on such a brave face; but there's nothing like humour to create a smokescreen.

'My father had the same diagnosis, Prof – and he lived for another nine years.' Sheila was initially adopting the comforting approach, though she knew how serious the Professor's situation was.

'Bertie said that you favoured an alternative approach to these things, Sheila. You know that I'm not into that sort of thing. I trust my doctor and the specialist.'

'That's important, Prof. I'm sure they're doing their best and with great skill. My interest', she went on, 'is in helping the body to do some work, too.'

'Like what?'

'Well, you've heard of the immune system, I'm sure. It's an extraordinary ability that the body has to keep at bay unhelpful intruders and to hold in balance the innumerable microorganisms that live inside us and that are essential to our physical health.'

Here we go, thought the Professor. Half-digested theories from some New Age book. If Sheila had known what he was thinking she would probably have teased him about his shelves of Old Age books.

'For all sorts of reasons, many of which we don't understand,' she continued, 'the body's ability to keep us healthy can become weakened, particularly as we get older.'

'So what do we do?' responded the Professor. 'If it's simply wear and tear that you're talking about, we can't just simply slip into another body. They told me the other day that my toaster wasn't worth repairing. I've had it twenty years or more. I'm not going to argue.'

'You're a little more complicated than a toaster, my dear Professor,' chipped in Bertie.

'Thank you for the compliment, my friend – but I'm not really. Parts wear out. Some are not replaceable. An obsolete model is what I am!'

'Prof, we're all going to die,' said Sheila. 'Nobody denies that; but what Bertie means is that maybe it's only our physical body that is mortal.'

'You know already what I believe, Prof,' said Bertie; 'and what encourages me in this belief is the sense that so many people have – and I certainly have it myself – that there's more to life than meets the eye, and that matter – what we can weigh and measure – is not the only reality. And it's not necessarily to do with a heaven somewhere else; it's just deeper layers and other dimensions of what surrounds us in our daily lives.'

'So what sort of help are you suggesting that the body – this immune system – needs?'

'Well, a good healthy diet and plenty of exercise are obvious answers,' was Sheila's initial response. 'Then there's a substance made from mistletoe that people I respect have spoken about. Apparently it can strengthen the immune system's efforts to arrest and even to eliminate cancer.'

'That's exactly what I thought. Druids, Aboriginals – it all belongs to the past,' responded the Professor. 'People believed in these things because they knew no better. We now have what's called science – things we can prove by experiment, and not just ideas we have to believe and trust.'

We've lost it, thought Bertie as the Professor thundered on, but he wasn't at all surprised. Nor indeed was Sheila, who knew only too well how very many so-called educated people tended to think these days. She knew, too, that one of the most important elements in healing – not healing just in terms of overcoming illness and avoiding death – was connected not to medicines and surgery, brilliant as they could sometimes be, but to what she'd heard described as the transmuted power of love. 'Love is the medicine we can give to one another' was a phrase she remembered reading somewhere.

She and Bertie and Bunny, and all the Professor's other friends in the village and elsewhere, would stand by him – of that she was sure – whatever differences existed between what each one of them believed about life and death and whether or not there was some deeper meaning to it all. It was out of this recognition of people's essential compassion for one another that Bertie, too, sought to reassure his troubled friend.

'Can I tell Bunny about your situation, Prof? She's so fond of you and will be very anxious to help.'

'I don't want to end my days swamped in apple crumble,' the Professor mumbled, though he was secretly touched that people seemed concerned about his situation. Above all he was fast becoming aware of how he needed company. For almost the first time in his life he no longer wanted to be alone.

'That's Bunny's way of caring,' went on Bertie. 'But it's the caring that will nourish you as much as the food.'

Despite the Professor's dismissive remarks about complementary med-icine, Sheila and Bertie were both touched by this gentler and more humorous person who was gradually emerging from his book-lined world of scholarship and single-minded routine.

After removing his spectacles and pausing to gaze around the room and at the view from his window, and finally into the faces of his friends, he replied, 'I suppose there's no point in trying to keep it a secret, particularly in a village like this. How's the Major, by the way?'

'He's a new man,' said Sheila proudly.

'Explain'.

'My Joey has unlocked a whole chest of secrets.'

'What secrets?'

'His career in the army. Did you know he was in a tank regiment and fought in the Korean War?'

'Had no idea. He's never mentioned it. Thank God I missed National Service. Wouldn't fancy shooting anyone. How about you, Bertie?'

'Too young; but boarding school was almost as bad. Just like those boys in *Lord of the Flies*, but no deaths – only because the bell used to go just in time.'

Later that day, as Bertie and Peggy were walking on the forest, she finally told him the story that she'd told to Bouncer. Bertie wasn't at all surprised and could already see how liberated his friend had become through sharing her secret. She'd been talking enthusiastically about starting a Book Club in the village and also of offering to help Bunny with some of the WI arrangements. Perhaps in time she would share with her, too, the story of why she had come to live in Hartfield with her godmother all those years ago.

Only as they started to head back towards the village did Bertie tell Peggy about the crisis in the Professor's life. That news immediately put any lingering worries she might have into perspective. She was healthy and in many ways led a charmed life. She was lonely sometimes, and occasionally haunted by the thought that she'd wasted her life, but as she left Bertie her overwhelming feeling was one of gratitude for being alive, and she was full of thoughts about how she might be of help to the Professor.

Bunny's response to the news had initially been somewhat different: it had prompted an underlying sense of her own vulnerability. Perhaps this is why I always keep myself so busy, she thought. But now suddenly the reality of death seemed to make everything else irrelevant. She felt even more in need to talk to Bertie again – the sort of conversation they'd started to have on the forest.

In the meantime she phoned the Professor and arranged to call by around six o'clock. There was nothing she could bring, she was told. 'Just your dear, busy self.'

Bunny's first reaction on seeing the Professor was surprise that he looked his normal self, though he did have a cut on his chin that she imagined was caused from shaving. But, apart from some cotton wool dangling from the wound, there was no outward sign that anything was wrong or different. Of course not, she thought; particularly with something like cancer, that silent and initially undetectable intruder that could destroy something as complex and miraculous as a human body.

'How are you feeling, Prof?' It was an obvious question to ask, even somewhat blunt; but Bunny wasn't going to pretend there wasn't a crisis.

'Strangely well,' he replied. 'No pain, but no doubt that will come'.

Bunny's immediate response was to tell him that he was starting to sound like the Major, but she stopped herself just in time. Instead of teasing, she stuck to what she hoped would be a helpful tack and a practical approach. That was certainly how the Professor's mind seemed to work – or had done so until now.

'They have wonderful drugs these days to alleviate pain, I'm told. But what about treatment? What are they offering?'

'Well, because the cancer has already spread, chemotherapy seems to be the only option, along with some hormone therapy. I'm not sure it's worth it. Feeling ghastly for weeks and with no guarantee that it will finally do the job.'

'I am sorry, Prof. I was devastated when Bertie told me. We take so much for granted, not least our health and the health of our friends.'

Bunny suddenly felt close to tears and turned towards the window that overlooked the village church and the forest beyond. The curtains had not yet been drawn, but it was dark outside. She was not the crying type, she told herself.

The Professor said nothing. For a change, he seemed to be listening rather than arguing. She sensed a chink in his armour of certainty.

'So much for granted,' she repeated wistfully, both to herself and to her silent friend. 'Tomorrow's sunrise, the postman, church bells on Sunday, water from the tap; above all the people we care about.'

She turned back to face just such a person; a bit of a loner like herself, but a loner who was probably starting to wish that he wasn't quite so alone.

But who knows, Bunny wondered, what is really going on in his mind? Who can know what any of us think and feel? Was he frightened, or possibly depressed? Perhaps he was embarrassed by that tear she felt running down her cheek; or was he longing for her to stop talking and to simply go away?

Chapter Twelve

In which Bunny and Bouncer plan an entertainment,
while Bertie reflects on autumn, sleep and death.

———————•———•———

For the next week or so, while the Professor tried to make up his mind about the treatments on offer, his friends increasingly rallied round. Peggy came to discuss her idea of a Book Club with him, Bouncer showed him the script of a play he'd been sent, and Sheila took him a tonic, with the promise that there was nothing weird in it.

Amid all this activity and concern, the threat of a bypass had almost been forgotten. No further meeting of the Action Group was planned, but Bunny and Bertie did go round to the Professor's house to bring their friend up to date with the latest news from the County Council about dates for a Public Consultation. Sir Christopher had also sent another handwritten note to say that the advice he'd been given was that they should summon up as much local support as possible prior to the Consultation. There had also been no further sight of the man with a tie and a tripod. The Professor, however, was more interested to know whether they'd given up looking for whorls along the proposed route, and was assured that the hunt would go on.

Bouncer and Bunny, meanwhile, continued their discussion about a Valentine's Day entertainment – *Heartaches in Hartfield* – but soon decided that there was too little time to get something so ambitious off the ground by February. Instead they would work on the idea over the coming year – script, music, and rummaging around in the village for hidden talent. Sheila was already in their sights; and little Peggy, who had recently shown signs of emerging from her shell, had been discussed as a possible Cinderella. Bouncer knew from experience that some of the best actors are quite shy people when not on stage. In the tradition of pure pantomime, he rather liked the idea of playing Sleeping Beauty himself; in which case Sheila would make a perfect Prince Charming.

'No point in casting it until we've written a script,' said the ever-practical Bunny, though she was increasingly swept along by Bouncer's enthusiasm and wild ideas.

Thanks to Joey and his toy tanks, Sheila's friendship with the Major had gone from strength to strength. A mended fuse box and a properly functioning electric fire had also helped to bring warmth not only to the house but also to their relationship. Now, on Wednesday afternoons, while Sheila was at her yoga class, Joey was taken round to play soldiers with his new friend.

On one such afternoon, while the sound of warfare echoed round the Major's end of the village, Bertie was on his way to tea with Bunny at the peaceful end of Hartfield. All that morning he'd been working on a new poem, and he was now looking forward to company, and above all to a slice or two of the coffee cake that Bunny had promised.

'I'm troubled by the thought that the Professor might not pull through, Bertie. Troubled by the thought of death in a way that I've never experienced before.'

The tea party was nearly over; so, too, they both knew, was the kind of chat that oils the wheels of daily life but often avoids what people are really thinking and feeling. Bunny had asked Bertie round not just to treat him to coffee cake, but because she was feeling more and more ill at ease and needed to talk about it.

'I'm not sure what to say, Bunny. Maybe listening is the most helpful thing I can do.'

'You said once that we're alarmed by death because we don't understand life. What did you mean? You talked to me on that walk about love and about overcoming our feeling of separateness. But then death, it seems to me, puts an end to it all.'

'Well, Bunny, I can only tell you a few of the thoughts that help me; but, as I've said before, they may not be thoughts that will help you.'

Let's try,' she said with a smile.

'Well, I think that our understanding of life has become very blinkered and too narrowly focussed, hence our fear of death. Our five senses are extraordinary and miraculous and allow us to navigate in the physical world. But what none of these senses reveals is the mystery of life itself, and nor do they tell us what our existence might mean.'

'Many people believe there is no meaning.'

'I know, and I can see why. But if you have a sense, as many people do, that there is so much else going on that seems to be hidden, then what starts to dawn on you is the realisation that something else will be necessary – alongside our eyes and ears and our fingertips – to at least glimpse these great mysteries of existence. It's as though a faculty is needed that can see behind what our senses reveal. Something that's more than just faith.'

'So what is this precious faculty, Bertie? What's wrong with the brain?'

'The brain, like the rest of our body, is mortal, Bunny; it will die. But if you imagine that this hidden world to which I'm referring exists outside of time and space – is infinite and eternal – then only something in us that corresponds to it, and is likewise eternal, can comprehend and relate to it. And this extra sense that I'm talking about is what might start to give us a window, if you like, into this deeper reality.'

'But what is it, if it's not the brain?' responded Bunny, who was making a huge effort to follow what her friend was trying to explain.

'It's like a baby in us that has yet to be born. You could also call it our potential, this journey I'm trying to describe,' he replied. 'It's what we talked about the other day.'

'That's the word they always use in schools – nurturing the child's potential,' said Bunny.

'True; and perhaps an essential aspect of our potential, as we grow up and as humanity evolves, is connected with what I'm talking about – to awaken what is dormant within us. But it involves work, just as learning to spell does.'

'What do you mean?'

'Well, much of what influences and informs us is taking place unconsciously; but it can manifest, for example, in this feeling that so many people have that we don't just cease to exist when we die. And perhaps the most important result of working to awaken this awareness to which I am referring will be our ability to gradually become more conscious of these other levels of reality.'

'Do you mean that we are already a lot wiser than we realise?'

'Yes, I do; and if we pay greater attention to what slumbers in our hearts and minds, and nurture it with a more contemplative approach to life, we may very gradually discover what lies behind the knowledge we've acquired through observation of the physical world and our purely intellectual interpretation of those observations.'

'And death?' Bunny asked.

'Well, as long as we think of life only in physical terms and as finite, then death is naturally forbidding and something to be feared. But if death is not an end, but instead an interval, just as sleep is – a sleep from which we wake each morning – then it is something to be welcomed, not dreaded. We need that pause, just as we need each night.'

'That I can understand, Bertie, but I still have a problem with this other faculty you're talking about.'

Bertie turned to look out of the bay window, not at the magnificent holly tree in Bunny's garden, but out beyond what his eyes revealed, as though searching for what he was seeing inwardly and for the words to describe it.

'We hear, but we don't always listen, Bunny. Listening requires effort, but if we do it more often – truly listen – we will gradually hear more.'

For a moment Bertie found himself thinking about his recent visit to

The Cedars, when the subject of the Professor's illness was first mentioned, and about all that had seemed to take place *between* the words – and even more so during the actual pauses in their conversation.

'The "sound of silence"', he said, 'is a wonderfully paradoxical phrase that an American monk called Thomas Keating spoke about.'

Bunny's first reaction was to recognise how little silence there was in her life, and how, when it did occur, she instinctively rushed to fill it. Yet what Bertie was saying also struck a deeper chord. She paused in response to what he was suggesting, and to honour this 'sound of silence'.

'I suppose you could say the same thing about looking,' she eventually said. 'We look at the world, but we don't always see.'

After a pause she added, 'Though we do sometimes say "I see what you mean". Is that a clue to what you're talking about?'

'Absolutely! And it's this activity – paying greater attention to all that surrounds us – that can slowly awaken our ability to see and hear more; it's what is meant by that word "seer".'

Bunny stumbled inwardly at the word 'seer', but was helped when Bertie then repeated it as 'see-er'.

It's what meditation is really all about,' he continued, 'but a meditation that we can then take into daily life; and if, in one form or another, we do it more often – be still and silent and listen and, in Goethe's words, 'allow nature to whisper her secrets to us' – I do believe that deeper truths will slowly emerge; truths that will enable us not only to better understand the world, and to live saner, kinder lives, but also to embrace death with the same equanimity that we welcome sleep after a hard day's work.'

Bertie paused, sensing that his companion needed a rest. He also imagined, rightly or wrongly, that these ideas were not what her friends and relations tended to talk or think about.

'More cake? More tea?' she asked.

'No, thank you.'

Bunny got up to draw the curtains. Soon it would be dark. Perhaps she should light the fire.

Not far away other people were also coming to terms with the arrival of autumn and drawing their curtains. Meanwhile on the forest the bracken was no longer green, the insects had largely disappeared, and life altogether seemed to be withdrawing. But what in many ways looked like death was – in the eyes of people like Bertie – simply a retreat underground and a period of energetic but invisible activity. To stay alive in the cold of winter involved something just as miraculous as the shapes and colours that would emerge again in the spring. It was this thought that he had tried to share with Peggy a few days ago, in an effort to lift the gloom she always felt at this time of year.

For people too, he felt, it was an opportunity to turn inwards after the expansion and breathing out that happens in summer. Nature had worked her miracles, and it was now our turn to be creative and to blossom. Sheila would soon start writing down the story she'd been telling Joey at bedtime. In it she had imagined the creatures and plants that lived in their garden talking to each other about human beings and trying to understand their funny ways. Bouncer, who flourished on fantasy, had been impressed by Sheila's creativity as a mother. Her story, he told her, was like a rare and beautiful fruit that had slowly ripened during those warm and sunny months.

What had blossomed for Bertie during the last two months, as the threat to their forest hung over him, was a deeper sense than ever of people's interconnectedness, not just with each other, but with the whole of nature. How to share this experience, and the urgency he felt, while at the same time recognising and respecting other people's cares and priorities, was the challenge he continually experienced.

'Please understand, Bunny, that I struggle with these ideas as much as everyone else.' The afternoon tea party was drawing to a close, but the conversation between Bertie and his old friend wasn't quite over.

'It's our fragility and doubts', he went on, 'that I hope prevent us – prevent me – from becoming fanatical. Certainty is the great trap. I don't *know* anything, Bunny. I've read some books, but, most importantly, I've tried increasingly to heed these words: "What is this life if, full of care, we have no time to stand and stare." Do you know the poem? It's by W. H. Davies. I must show it to you.'

'Thank you, Bertie,' responded Bunny, though she was still aware of her tenuous relationship with poetry. 'But if what you're saying is true,' she continued, 'then …'

'No, "true" is too strong a word; it's intimations that I occasionally experience.'

'All right, intimations then. Anyway, the implication behind what you're saying is that most of us are only half awake; and that the ability to see more is – what was the word you used? – yes, dormant. If so, Bertie, what is it that will help to wake us up?'

'Perhaps sorrow: sorrow that the Professor is dangerously ill; sorrow at the hurt we cause other people; sorrow that so many people in the world suffer. But it doesn't mean we have to go round with long faces all the time. Joy is a healing force, too: joy that the forest exists, that my bees work so selflessly to produce the miracle that is honey; joy that the Major is enjoying the company of little Joey; joy that Peggy has started to shake off her troubled past; and joy that you, Bunny, have become such good friends with Bouncer.'

Bunny was touched by these last words. She knew that her life, or rather what went on in her head – what someone like Bertie would call her inner life – had been changing significantly in the past month or so.

'What's made *you* think so deeply about these things, Bertie?' she asked him.

'I don't talk much about my past, as you know, Bunny. I suppose it's partly because I feel that the past and the present are not really so separate; and the degree to which I live fully in the moment, in the now, is for me almost as though I exist outside of time. But to answer your question, there was – there is – a wound I carry that I am still trying to understand and to heal.'

Despite her relatively comfortable existence, Bunny had seen enough of life to know about wounds, including some of her own. But she tried not to let those memories distract her from what Bertie was saying.

'A couple of years after I left school there was an accident, a car crash,' he continued, 'and my mother was killed. The loss was devastating. "Where is she now?" I asked myself. It's a question that has never gone away, and as a result I've always felt a very strong connection to people who are no longer alive physically – and not just to my mother.'

Bunny thought of her own parents, and of her sister who'd died as a child. Perhaps they were more present in her life than she realised – and not just as a memory.

'And your father?' she asked.

'I never knew him. No pain there – at least not for me.'

Bunny waited. For a moment Bertie closed his eyes, then he turned to his companion with a faraway look that she'd never quite witnessed before.

'People sometimes say that time heals,' he went on, as details of his own mother's tragic death resurfaced under Bunny's sympathetic gaze, 'but that tends to imply that you gradually forget and that life takes over. My own understanding, which has taken many years to arrive at, is that the healing comes from the fact that we are not actually separate from those who have died.'

'That's not how it seems to most people.'

'I agree, but, as I was saying earlier, maybe that's because what I'm talking about is, for most of us, largely unconscious. Perhaps at night, when we fall asleep and the nature of consciousness changes, we are united with them. You know that sleep has been traditionally called "the little death".'

'That sounds a bit grim!'

'Not if you stop thinking of death as an end.'

'I suppose not; but you know what I mean.'

'Of course.'

'And where does all this take place? Are you simply talking about heaven? And why don't we remember?'

'Perhaps we don't remember, in the usual sense of the word, because our exile – if I can use that word – is meaningful for our spiritual evolution; but that doesn't mean we aren't touched by these unconscious experiences. Anyway I don't think of this existence, this space between one day and the next, between one incarnation and another, as somewhere else. For me heaven, and indeed the experience of hell, is here – sometimes visible, sometimes not.'

'And your mother's invisible?'

'If you like; but so, too, is the essential me. And while my body sleeps, so I like to imagine, the essential me continues to experience my mother's love, in a way distinct from a daytime memory. And perhaps it's these blessings, these bonds, that enable us – to a far greater extent than we realise – to cope with the ups and downs of daily life.'

The church clock struck six. Bertie stood up and tried not to spill the crumbs from his cake onto the floor. It was now dark outside. He'd said enough. Bunny fetched him his coat.

'I hope your mother was listening,' she said as she gave her friend a hug.

'I hope so, too. And maybe, night after night, I also bring something helpful to her from this funny old place in which we find ourselves. Who knows?'

CHAPTER THIRTEEN

*In which Peggy has a worrying dream,
and the Professor helps the Major to use the Internet*

———————•———•———

The November frosts continued to bring a new beauty to the Forest, with patches of white lingering where the sun hadn't managed to reach, and the red of the rowan berries defying the effect that the cold was gradually inflicting on the life around them.

For some people, however, the experience of nature, whether it be the thrill and colour of spring, or the stillness and sparkle of winter, can bring home to them how pale and unspectacular they are in comparison. This was Peggy's mood as she made her way to post her completed form about single occupancy and her Council Tax. She felt even more alone and depleted having found that Bertie wasn't at home, and knowing that Bouncer had gone to London for the day.

The relief that she'd recently experienced through unburdening herself to Bouncer, and then to Bertie, seemed to be fading fast. It was the feeling of rejection that she still couldn't quite shake off. Her visit to the Professor to discuss her idea of a Book Club had not been a success. He'd told her that he hardly ever read novels, and anyway preferred to keep his reactions to himself. She imagined that his illness, which was now no secret, might be affecting his attitude to everything and not just to her initiative; but his response had nevertheless undermined her fragile self-confidence. Even her offer to shop for him was turned down. 'I'm not an invalid yet,' had been his rather insensitive response. It was nothing personal, she told herself, but in her mind it was another reminder of how little she mattered to others.

Bunny, too, hadn't welcomed her offer to help with the WI with much enthusiasm. She'd been perfectly polite, but Peggy needed encouragement. At least she had Bertie as a friend, she thought. And maybe Bouncer could cheer her up when he got back from London.

On top of all these worries, last night she'd had a very vivid dream that was still haunting her. In it she'd been driving around in the little blue Polo she used to own, but she was frantically looking for that same car that she was in. She imagined that someone like Bouncer's wise grandfather would have been able to explain the dream to her; or maybe Bouncer could.

That same afternoon the Major made one of his rare visits to The Cedars; in fact he rarely visited anyone. The Professor, who'd been trying to do some work on his half-finished book, was pleased to see his old friend and welcomed the interruption. He was due to see his consultant in a couple of days and was finding it hard to concentrate on anything apart from his growing sense of 'the enemy within'. He was pleased, too, that the Major hadn't come armed with all sorts of worrying facts and figures about cancer, now that the news was out.

In fact the purpose of the visit, apart from a sincere but unspoken gesture of sympathy, was to ask for help with his computer. The Major seldom used it, except sometimes to check the weather forecasts or the stock market. His newspaper, along with the radio, gave him all the news he wanted to hear.

Now suddenly he faced a new challenge. Sheila had told him that next week was Joey's sixth birthday and he wanted to respond. He had no close relatives of his own and was certainly unaware of any children who even knew of his existence. He'd heard about eBay from Bertie, who had bought several of his beehives that way. What the Major had wondered was whether he could find a large model tank – preferably a Centurion – to give to Joey as a birthday present. However, what keys or buttons to press on his computer had been beyond him.

The Professor had never used eBay, but had no problem finding it. They scrolled through masses of offers, but one in particular caught the Major's eye. It was a splendid model of a Centurion tank, but much larger than Joey's two toys. It also came with a remote control that not only enabled it to go backwards and forwards, but also allowed you to raise and lower the gun and to revolve the turret.

Even the Professor, a committed pacifist ever since the Vietnam War, was impressed. They submitted a generous offer, and for a few brief moments the two old friends were transported back into their largely forgotten childhoods.

As the Major was leaving, however, the mood changed rapidly when he noticed his missing umbrella in the stand by the front door.

'So sorry, old boy,' was the Professor's somewhat sheepish response. 'Someone must have accidentally picked it up and then left it here without thinking.'

When Bouncer got back from London, Sheila had just finished putting Joey to bed. He felt that his meeting had gone well, but he was also well aware that he worked in an increasingly crowded profession and that several other actors were probably feeling just as hopeful. Theatre work was notoriously badly paid, so something for television – even if it was as banal as a commercial – would be very welcome.

'Where's your family, Bouncer?' Sheila asked him as they settled down by the fire with a simple supper. Sheila had been a vegetarian for some years, but had no problem with Bouncer munching away on a huge bacon sandwich.

'My father died quite a few years ago, and my mother lives near my sister and her family up north.'

'Where up north?'

'Near Skipton in Yorkshire. My sister's a head teacher in a primary school.'

'Are you close?'

'In a way. We quarrelled like hell as kids, but I suppose that's normal.'

'I think brothers and sisters are important for that very reason,' Sheila said. 'They rub the rough edges off one another. I'm worried that Joey's an only child.'

'He'll survive. We all survive. There's no perfect formula, no perfect childhood.'

'Is it chance, Bouncer? Do you think life's just chance?'

'I doubt it. There's destiny, so some believe, weaving itself in and out of people's lives from day to day; blessings and challenges; unexpected knocks on the door.'

'Like yours on mine!'

'That's right; but we don't have to answer the door! I was talking to Peggy about all this the other day. They call it karma in India. "May I want the life I've chosen" is how one wise chap described the challenge.'

'Do you mean we've made choices before we're born?'

'That's the implication – to try to put right the mess we made last time. And there are probably some things that we can't simply wash down the sink and forget about – or should want to.'

In this lifetime, too, was Sheila's immediate thought.

'I read a wonderful book recently called *Bird Brain*,' went on Bouncer. 'It was about a terrible English gent who was passionate about pheasant shooting, but not much else. Then one day, at some grand shoot on his estate, his gun blows up and he's killed. But then he's reincarnated as a pheasant …'

'As a pheasant?' Sheila interrupted rather incredulously.

'Yes, and his whole aim is then not only to find out who tinkered with his gun, but also to try and put right the relationships he neglected during his lifetime. There are advantages and disadvantages in being a pheasant, all of which are hilariously described, but the essential message is that it's never too late. And it's relationships that are crucial.'

Bouncer paused, and for a moment Sheila looked away, away into the years before her arrival in England. Bouncer, too, found himself suddenly thinking about his own past. His next remark was directed as much to himself as it was to Sheila.

'And it's often the difficult relationships that I believe are the most crucial ones of all. It's how we grow and learn. Karma is largely about relationships.'

'You sound very certain about the idea, Bouncer!'

'I'm not really. But somewhere among all those age-old teachings there's something that makes sense to me.'

Sheila suddenly felt a huge surge of gratitude that chance, or whatever it was, had brought Bouncer knocking on her door.

'It reminds me of something that someone back in Australia said to me years ago about life as a challenge to remember what we've forgotten. Perhaps they meant from past lives.'

'Maybe they did,' said Bouncer. 'But the theory can tend to overshadow the idea of learning something new in this lifetime. My problem with the traditional idea of karma is that it can create a kind of fatalism. If you're born into rotten circumstances it's what you deserve, but if you do a good job as a sweeper without complaining you'll get a better deal next time – in your next life.'

'You mean the caste system?'

'Exactly. We had just the same system here in the Western world, but we called it "knowing your place".'

'And it hasn't totally disappeared, even in Australia.'

At that moment Joey called out from the bedroom; it turned out that a moth was trapped in the lampshade by his bed. Was this just chance, wondered Sheila, or had something far wiser than the three of them decided that the conversation was over?

Bouncer returned to his half-eaten bacon sandwich, and Sheila also welcomed the pause. A deep discussion – however inspiring – like everything else in life had its right moment and duration and needed to be balanced, even by something as mundane as a moth or a bacon sandwich.

CHAPTER FOURTEEN

*In which Peggy makes a discovery,
and Bunny has a problem with her doves.*

————————————•———•———

Peggy woke the next morning feeling elated, and all because of a quite different dream. In this one there had been no feeling of anxiety, just pure joy. The details were fading fast, but what she remembered above all was the phrase she was uttering as she woke up: 'I want to dance in the sky.'

As a child she used to have what she called her 'flying dreams', and last night that blissful experience of being totally free of gravity had recurred. What did it mean? And why now? Was something or someone trying to cheer her up? Perhaps it was just wise Peggy trying to cheer up timid Peggy.

Her immediate instinct was to share the dream with Bertie, but then she remembered that it was his day as a volunteer with a charity that helped refugees and asylum-seekers to speak and read English. She knew anyway how difficult it is to communicate one's dreams to another person; she'd tried it occasionally. The details sounded absurd, and the powerful feelings that one experienced were almost impossible to convey. Perhaps that's what poets, artists and composers can do, she thought.

Instead Peggy decided to go on a hunt for whorls on her own. A few days ago, when she'd still been feeling cheerful and confident, she'd contacted a charity called Buglife which had been involved in the Newbury snail saga. It was on her own initiative entirely, and as yet she'd told no one, not even Bertie. Her intention was to take the new information that they'd given her to the next meeting; but meanwhile why not have another search on her own with no conversations to distract her?

Autumn was a good time to look for snails, before the winter inevitably depleted their numbers, so a Buglife spokesman had told her. They had been right to concentrate on damp areas beside the many streams that criss-crossed the forest, particularly where there were reeds growing.

It was a beautiful, sunny day, and despite the wind it was warm enough to leave scarf and gloves behind. Still glowing from the experience of her dream, Peggy made for an area that she felt had not yet been thoroughly explored.

She wasn't exactly dancing, and certainly had her two feet firmly on the ground, but in other ways she was feeling as free and light as the buzzard who swooped and swerved overhead. A tortoiseshell butterfly, seemingly unaware that the summer was over, flew across her path. She'd always loved butterflies, and remembered how when she was a small child her father, despite his busy life as a farmer, took time to tell her their names. She also remembered him saying that butterflies were like flowers released from their stems.

Bunny was having a far less euphoric day than Peggy. In fact she was in what some would call 'a right old stew'; and so much so that she had left the actual stew that she'd cooked for the Professor far too long in the oven. At least some of it could be rescued, she told herself. A tin of chopped tomatoes would soon moisten up what at the moment looked decidedly unappetising.

The distraction had come from next door, where her neighbours had yet again been complaining about her doves. For some unaccountable reason the birds had started to use the neighbours' courtyard as their lavatory, and the mess was appalling.

Bunny had phoned Bertie, him being someone who knew a bit about animals – or at least about bees. Both bees and doves fly, she told herself, so there must be some connection.

The toilet habits of doves turned out to be outside Bertie's area of expertise, but the crisis prompted a visit, followed by a much more interesting conversation.

Bunny had often wondered which one of her doves determined when and where they went on their periodic flights together; which one was the boss? And why did they never bump into each other on those flights?

'Birds never do,' said Bertie, 'but nor, on the whole, do we – even on a crowded pavement.'

'So which one is the leader then? Which one makes the decisions?'

'Maybe none of them! It's like saying which of my legs, the right one or the left one, decides to go for a walk.'

'So you mean they're obeying some great hidden dove who's in charge of them?'

'Maybe.'

'You like that word, don't you, Bertie!'

Her friend grinned.

'I use it because I don't know the answer to your question, Bunny. All I can do is imagine.'

Bertie then turned to look out of the window as Bunny's flock of doves flew past on their afternoon adventure. Yes, in flight they certainly do seem to be one, rather than twenty or so individual birds, thought Bunny.

'Thank you, doves, for encouraging us to wonder,' Bertie called out softly as the birds disappeared behind the church tower.

But another voice, far less soft, then came from over Bunny's wall. The neighbours wanted a meeting. She was glad she had Bertie with her, even though he clearly had no solution in mind.

'Live and let live' was Bertie's motto, which is why he never dug up the molehills in his garden or removed the stinging nettles that grew happily outside his back door.

'Lucky for you that moles do their business underground' might have been Bunny's response, had she known what he was thinking.

Peggy couldn't hear the voice of Bunny's neighbour, but nor could any of them hear the gasp of surprise and delight that she had uttered just minutes before.

On the edge of a small pond, and sheltered by reeds, she had suddenly discovered, after hours of patient searching, a whole colony of Desmoulin's whorl snails – totally unaware of how special they were and what power they possessed.

The warm sunshine had disappeared hours ago, but she had stayed on the forest despite the sudden change in the weather. Now in her small hand, pink from the cold, nestled one very bewildered snail. Peggy had with her the photograph that the Professor had printed out from the Internet, and this tiny creature undoubtedly belonged to the species named in honour of the French naturalist Charles des Moulins.

As she sat on the grass beside the pond, gazing in wonder at this tiny, beautiful and perfect creature, she began to feel enormously encouraged that human beings, despite their ingenuity and technical achievements, recognised that a humble snail actually mattered and was of importance. Indeed it had just as much right to live quietly by this pond as we have to walk in the woods, build factories, write poetry or simply wonder what it all might mean. Suddenly much of what Bertie had talked about for years, and which she had only ever half understood, made huge sense to her.

Despite the cold and the damp grass she was in no hurry to move, or to rush home and tell everyone the news. She was also hesitant about taking one of the snails away from its home, and yet she knew that was what she had to do. At least she would look after it carefully, and, hopefully, it could be returned to the forest, once a lot of clever people had weighed, measured and photographed it and then formally identified it as a rare type of snail.

And if any of the other creatures on the forest happened to be watching this small human creature gazing at an even smaller creature, they may well have assumed – being not well versed in biology – that this was a mother with her child, such was the tenderness with which Peggy nursed her tiny whorl.

CHAPTER FIFTEEN

In which Bertie gets a shoe full of water,
and Bunny decides to slow down.

'I saw something yesterday that made me really glad that I live in the UK.'

Bouncer laughed at Sheila's cheerful greeting as he joined her for a late Sunday morning breakfast. Joey had already finished, and was busy drawing a picture of a centipede fighting with a ladybird.

'What was it? No, let me guess … the vicar on his bicycle.'

'Wrong!'

Bouncer grinned and then gazed up at the ceiling in search of an even more endearing image of England in all its quirkiness. In fact he'd only seen the vicar a couple of times, whereas Sheila – though not a churchgoer – had recently made friends with him.

In fact the Professor and Bunny were the only two people that Sheila knew who went regularly to church; but in her mind there were lots of other ways that people knelt in awe – not always literally – and in gratitude for the miracles that surrounded them. Bertie was certainly one of those kneelers; in fact his whole life seemed to her a kind of hymn to the joys and sacredness of life – his bees, his friends, the stars, his chocolate biscuits.

'I know,' said Bouncer. 'That old lady who wheels her ancient dog around in a pram.'

'Good guess, but not the right one.' Sheila was enjoying the game, and Joey had also started to listen.

'Was it that box full of rather tired-looking apples, outside the cottage next to the Major's hovel, with the sign "Help yourself"?'

'What's a hovel?' asked Joey.

'It's a house that needs sorting out, and we're helping to do that, aren't we Joey? So "hovel" is the wrong word and the box of apples is the wrong guess!'

'I give up.' Bouncer pulled a sad face that made Joey laugh.

'All right, I'll tell you. I was waiting at a bus stop in Tunbridge Wells yesterday, and a bus went by with a notice on the front saying "Sorry, not in service". It was the "Sorry" that I loved.'

'Sorry, I want a biscuit,' said Joey. Fortunately, it was Sunday – the day for treats – so his wit was rewarded by the famous actor who sometimes went to

London and whose grandfather had lived in a jungle.

While Sheila was playing guessing games with Bouncer, Peggy was on her way to Bertie's house, clutching a small plastic box lined with mud and leaves which contained her precious snail. So far she'd spoken to no one. She had spent yesterday evening making as comfortable a home as she could for her tiny visitor.

Bertie was as thrilled as she was, and agreed that it looked exactly like the illustration on the Internet. Peggy had even dared to imagine her photograph in the local paper; and maybe that nice man on *The Guardian* who writes about ecology would interview her.

She and Bertie decided that they'd telephone Peggy's contact at Buglife first thing in the morning. An official identification was essential before the discovery was made public.

'But we must tell Bunny and the others,' said Bertie. 'They'll understand the importance of keeping quiet until we're certain.'

With no time to waste and breakfasts abandoned, Peggy took Bertie, together with Bunny, to the spot where she'd found her snail. It took a while to find any more snails, but it was finally Bertie, by now with one shoe full of water, who made the discovery. For once Bunny, who'd never really looked closely at a snail in her life, was lost for words; instead she gave both of them a warm hug.

'Now you must excuse me, or I'll be late for church.'

'Thank the Management on our behalf,' said Bertie. He almost felt like joining her, but he had his own private ritual on Sunday mornings. To an outsider it would appear to be an hour-long silence, eyes closed, no words. For Bertie the silence soon became another sort of existence – an existence in which those who had died were as real and as present as the people he saw and cared about every day; and he didn't want this experience to be interrupted by hymns, much as he loved them, or by announcements from the vicar about the state of the church roof.

The problem with the church roof, and how to raise the money for its repair, had been one of the Professor's concerns, and he was chairman of the group that had been formed to solve the problem; but he was fast withdrawing from such commitments.

That afternoon he had another surprise visit from the Major, but not this time for help with his computer. In fact the Major was deeply concerned about his friend's health; but in a very English, or rather an Englishman's, way, he was reluctant to actually say so. To show concern without words, let alone a hug, bewildered Bunny, as well as Sheila and Peggy and indeed Bouncer; but the Professor understood completely what was being silently communicated, and was touched that his reclusive and eccentric friend had even bothered to come round.

He'd also noticed how the Major had seemed to soften recently, but again – as a man of a certain age and background – he wouldn't dream of mentioning it. What he did suddenly remember was something that Sheila, in her somewhat forthright manner, had said about the Major when she was first getting to know him: 'I reckon he needs spraying with some WD-40 to loosen up those rusty bits.' Now he suddenly wanted to say to Sheila that perhaps that's what Joey, in all innocence, had actually done.

While all these thoughts went on in the Professor's head, he was talking away about what, until recently, he had always felt mattered – topics like social history and politics, good wine and the Ashes. But did they matter? Since the news of his diagnosis, and having digested the implications, he had noticed a shift taking place in his own priorities, and therefore in what he really wanted and indeed needed to discuss. But the Major – even with his rusty bits a little less rusty – was not the sort of person with whom he felt that he could really share these thoughts. Their relationship was close, but too established and set in its ways.

A person like Sheila was different. She was someone new in his life. There were fewer preconceptions, and, despite her strange medicines and her outrageous jokes, she was refreshingly open-minded and really seemed to listen. Bertie also listened, but there was a difference. The Professor had started to think about his parents, and about his mother in particular, which he hadn't done for years. Was it, perhaps, that Sheila was a woman that made him want to talk to her?

That afternoon, Bunny made a firm decision not to make any new lists until Monday and, more importantly – and more challenging – not to look at her smartphone until the evening at the earliest. She'd only bought it in the summer, and, despite its obvious usefulness, it had already become a very seductive magnet, taking up far too much of her time. On it she could find out what the weather was like in Edinburgh or in New Orleans, who invented umbrellas, and the current value of her stocks and shares. But she'd also found herself bombarded with information, offers and requests, as well as messages from people whom she had no deep desire to see again – all of it a distraction from what she liked to feel was really important.

But what was important? How would the Major, for example, answer that question? He'd probably say, 'Being able to pay the bills, staying healthy and making as few enemies as possible.' Or *would* he – if you really pinned him down, and especially after a glass or two of wine? What were *his* secret dreams and hopes? Surely he must have some; everyone does.

One of Bunny's long-standing resolves had been to start working her way through the pile of books, most of them recommended by Bertie, that had been accumulating on the table by the window. But most pressing of all was her plan to start playing the piano again, and to stop using the excuse that she was too busy or out of practice.

What had been gradually dawning on her, partly because of all that had happened in the past month or so – the threat of a bypass, the arrival of Bouncer, her recent conversations with Bertie and now the discovery of what might be an actual colony of whorl snails – was that her busyness was something she imposed on herself and was probably an escape from her more demanding aspirations. It was the same problem with the trivial television programmes that she knew were trivial, but couldn't turn off.

As a child Bunny had loved music, but as a teenager she had gradually become restless and too easily distracted to practise. By the time she was sixteen and shipped off to a smart finishing school, any plans to actually study music had been abandoned. Instead she learnt how to cook and arrange flowers, and how to darn socks for the prince who would soon appear to carry her off to his castle.

But the piano was still there, well polished but seldom played. As she settled down on that same stool that she remembered spinning around on as a little girl, she felt relieved that there was no one to listen – except perhaps her doves outside the window. Yet as she started to play – just some simple pieces by Ravel that she'd always loved – she found herself thinking about loneliness. Was this perhaps the real reason behind her constant busyness? Were all the obligations she felt towards her various causes, and to her friends and relations, actually a substitute for a close commitment to any one person? And if so, why? There had been a few close friendships when she was young, including the disastrous one, but none had lasted. Perhaps it was simply her destiny, whatever that is. It's what Bertie probably believed; also that strange fellow Bouncer, with his mysterious Bengali roots and talk about karma.

Bunny then remembered how a widowed friend had written to her recently saying that now there was nobody to do nothing with. The thought had made her sad – sad not just for her friend, but also briefly for herself.

'I wonder what Ravel thought about it all,' she wondered. 'Was *he* lonely?' She knew nothing about him or his life, although biography had always been one of her interests.

Among the books waiting to be read was one about Bertie's great hero, Leo Tolstoy, as well as a collection of his short stories.

Bunny played for a while longer, then made herself a cup of tea, avoided the dreaded phone and settled down by the fire to read one of her books. She felt peaceful and happy – happy in a way that she hadn't experienced for months, even years. I will try to hold onto this mood when I go to see the Professor in the morning, she told herself.

A Sunday afternoon in winter, with French music, a Russian tale, and tea from India; and thus for a few hours this quiet corner of an English village became home to the whole world.

Chapter Sixteen

In which Joey has a birthday party,
and Sheila tries to comfort the Professor.

———————•——•——•———————

When Peggy phoned her contact at Buglife the next morning she was told he was in a meeting until lunchtime. She'd checked her snail and it seemed to be alive. Whether it was well or not was impossible to tell, but at least it had been treated to some fresh mud and reeds for breakfast.

Peggy then remembered that it was Joey's birthday; there was an invitation to tea at four o'clock. Perhaps by then she would be feeling more relaxed, though still excited. She'd made Joey a large and colourful toy spider out of pipe cleaners. Her mother used to make all sorts of creatures like that at Christmas and hang them on the tree. Peggy did have a few such vivid and happy memories from her childhood, but it all felt a long time ago. She still had family in Devon, and although she hardly ever saw them, she always tried to remember their birthdays.

With Bunny and Bertie informed about the frustrating phone call, and undeterred by the Professor's previous rebuttal, she went round to see if he needed any shopping or help in the house. The Professor had already had an early morning visit from a slightly more serene Bunny, but all he'd really noticed was her strange-looking stew that had totally put him off his breakfast.

On the way to The Cedars, Peggy had met Bouncer looking rather glum. He'd just heard from his agent that the commercial he'd auditioned for had gone to someone else. Slight regrets about the pantomime offer he'd turned down back in the summer were beginning to surface. On the other hand, he thought to himself, if I was miles away in Manchester painting my nose bright red every evening, and twice on Wednesdays and Saturdays, I'd be missing my new friends in Hartfield and unable, perhaps, to be of some help to the Professor.

Bouncer had lived happily all over the place for years and never settled anywhere. But since arriving in this village he'd slowly started to feel the urge to stay put – at least for a while. Perhaps he should get a sensible job, whatever that was.

He'd sometimes wondered about teaching. He liked children, but had a feeling that the rules and regulations in a school – and above all the endless targets – would drive him mad. Surely every child's target was unique to them.

For one particular boy or girl to learn to read or write, or even simply to tie their own shoelaces, was just as significant an achievement as another child getting into Oxbridge.

Long ago he'd read about a school where none of the lessons was compulsory. The theory was that children naturally like to learn. If they don't want to go to school then there must be something wrong with the lessons. Nevertheless, he realised that some things in life are chores and have to be faced. For children, too, it's the same. Spelling has to be learnt, clothes kept tidy – but it can be fun, or that's what he remembered from his own childhood. It certainly seemed to be so for Joey.

Bertie was spending the morning strolling alone on the forest, with no particular route in mind. He loved the landscape at this time of year – the changing colour of the bracken, the mauve of the heather; but today it was the clouds that attracted his attention. Their different shapes started to remind him of people. Like clouds, he thought, we too are continually changing, yet shaped by so much more than the weather. But shaped by what? No one person is identical to another; no story ever the same.

At this moment a large grey cloud – it was tempting to think of it as the Major – moved into place between where Bertie was standing and the sun. The light changed; the view was suddenly different. Some colours faded, while in the distance the sunlight now fell upon his beloved clump of pine trees. Even dark and forbidding clouds should be welcomed, so he thought at that moment.

For several days he'd had been trying to write a poem about the Christmas story. It was a festival he loved and it was only a few weeks away, but he'd found himself stuck. Not the first poet to get stuck, he told himself; and so he walked and waited. Perhaps the poem already exists and I've just got to be in the right place for it to find me; that was an idea he remembered from somewhere.

The problem with Christmas, he felt, was the accumulation of clichés and preconceptions. Tradition was comforting and in many ways helpful, but it tended to stifle new insights and experiences.

What Bertie wanted to express in his poem was that *every* baby, and not just Jesus, is a miracle; a child's birth was also the opportunity for something new to be born into the world. The thought he then wanted to convey was that each new baby is not only a child of its parents but also a child of God – a birth that transcended physical procreation. Is that why people used to speak to children of a stork bringing the new baby? Children knew perfectly well that a baby grew in their mummy's tummy, but they were wise and innocent enough not to be troubled by the seeming contradiction of two different forms of arrival – a spiritual as well as a physical birth.

At two o'clock Peggy – the strong and confident Peggy – spoke to someone else at Buglife who promised to come down and investigate later in the week. She then hurried round to get Bertie, just back from his walk, but as yet with only a few words on paper, and together they went to tell Bunny the latest news.

After a quick cup of coffee, and a treat for the doves to try to keep them on Bunny's side of the wall, the three of them went on to the party together – a party that was outwardly to celebrate Joey's sixth birthday, but was also what they hoped might be a secret celebration for the Action Group.

The Professor had sent his apologies and good wishes, but the Major was there on the dot of four o'clock, clutching a huge parcel. Sheila was proud that Joey didn't rush from present to present, but took in and appreciated what everyone had brought. Fortunately the Major's parcel was the last to be opened, for nothing could then compete with the fearsome-looking tank. The two soldiers, together with Joey's young friend from the village, started to play with it happily, and Bouncer was allowed a quick go.

While the battle raged, Sheila treated the others to a large coffee cake she'd made in the shape of Australia, on top of which was a rather ropey-looking snail made of marzipan. The first slice, plus a portion of snail, was put aside for the Professor. Meanwhile Bertie, having devoured a slightly larger portion of both cake and snail – and while Sheila was in the kitchen and Bouncer was having another go with the tank – quietly agreed with Bunny and Peggy that a suitable climax to the party would be a visit by everyone to see a very real snail in its temporary home on a windowsill in Peggy's porch.

Later that evening, with Joey safely in bed and Bouncer babysitting, Sheila went round to see the Professor, taking him his treat from the party. He'd already heard the news of the snail from Bunny, and then from Peggy herself, but still wasn't quite convinced.

'Are you sure it's the right one?' he asked. 'There are over a hundred different species of snail in the UK alone.'

'We've all seen it,' she reassured him, 'and it's exactly like that picture from the Internet that you gave us.'

There was a pause. Did he now want to be left alone? Sheila noticed that the clock on his mantelpiece had stopped, but she didn't say anything. Was he still coping? She'd never been upstairs, but, as far as she knew, neither had any of his other visitors. She imagined the same sort of order as downstairs, with everything neatly in place: shoes all polished and in a row, shirts folded and ties hanging in a certain order. She wondered what books he kept by his bed. Perhaps there was even a Bible, read by the man whom no one really knew; the man who deep down was perhaps aware that his knowledge and his string of academic achievements were at times like a suit of armour, protecting him from those gentle arrows that Bertie, in particular, occasionally lobbed into his fortress.

'So, how have you been, Prof?'

'Not so good, to be honest. I've decided against any of the treatments.'

'That's brave.'

'Or cowardly, depending on your starting point.'

'And what's yours?'

'Acceptance. I've had a good life, though I probably won't finish this latest book.'

'I'm sure you will, Prof; and anyway, us human beings – do you really think we're ever finished?' asked Sheila. 'Resting maybe, but never finished.'

'I've said what I think. I'm not suddenly going to start believing the sort of stuff that you and Bertie believe. Even that fellow Bouncer seems to have his head full of ideas that went out of the window when people started to see reason.'

'Reason doesn't give us answers to the really big questions.'

'It will, you wait and see, and it will be science, not religion and mysticism, that will continue to help us forward.'

Maybe a science that also takes seriously what cannot be weighed and measured, thought Sheila; but she didn't want to get into that sort of argument with someone who, despite appearing outwardly as strong and as argumentative as ever, in all probability was inwardly feeling fragile and even somewhat insecure.

Instead she repeated very tentatively the thought that she'd shared with Bouncer some days ago: namely that humanity had done a lot of forgetting over the past hundred years or so, and maybe needed to do some remembering.

The Professor seemed uninterested or unwilling to discuss the idea, yet clearly wanted to continue their conversation.

'That strange lodger of yours, Bouncer – I think he was trying to be helpful and take my mind away from what's really going on – lent me a play that he'd been sent by his agent. As far as I can see it's meant to be addressing one of those big questions of yours. Doesn't stand a chance in my opinion, except in an upstairs room in some obscure London pub; but I'll try and be tactful in my response.'

'What's it about?'

'It's called – wait a minute, here it is – it's called *The Church Path*. The first act is set around the middle of the nineteenth century. And in those days, when most footpaths led to the church and most people walked, such paths were important thoroughfares.'

'And?'

'Well, there are all sorts of disputes going on in the village, disputes about rights of way and that sort of thing; even about the possibility of banning people who don't go to church from using the path. But what the play seems basically to be saying is that this church path is not really the problem, but has become the focus of people's difficulties and quarrels with one another. The issue divides the village, and in doing so reveals the underlying prejudices and antipathies that everyone carries.'

'Sounds interesting,' said Sheila.

'Yes, that part is all right. But in my opinion the second act goes completely off the rails.'

'Go on. Why?'

'Well, we're now in the present day, but in the same location, and the characters we met in Act 1 are also there, but in a different guise. The Victorian rector is now the gardener to the wealthy couple living at the Old Rectory; in the first act they were two troublesome farm labourers; and the dispute this time is about the couple's wish to move the footpath that runs past their house in order to have greater privacy. And so it goes on – rows with the neighbours, rows with the Church, rows with the Council – but why it has to bring in this mad notion of reincarnation beats me.'

'Why not?' responded Sheila. 'Maybe our problems with one another *do* continue until we learn some sense …'

'… and tolerance and empathy,' added the Professor, surprising Sheila, and indeed himself, that for a moment he was actually taking the play seriously and not just dismissing it as clumsy vehicle to preach weird ideas from the East.

'What would you like to be next time, if you had another life?'

'Steady on, Sheila! You're not trying to trap me into that fantasy, are you?'

'Of course not,' said Sheila with a smile. 'It's just a game.'

A game, in fact, was just what the Professor needed, she thought. And how wise of life – in this and in many other situations – to bring about such playful moments, despite the fog of facts and figures with which we constantly surround ourselves.

'A train driver!' volunteered her wrinkled playmate. 'No, not really; not on today's railways. But to me when I was young, like hundreds of other little boys, a steam engine was almost as exciting as a spacecraft is today. So maybe an astronaut.'

'I'd like to be composer,' said Sheila. 'You like music, Prof, don't you?'

'Classical, yes. Schubert in particular.'

'I was reading about Beethoven recently. I find it amazing that he could go on composing after he became totally deaf. It seems as though music can exist even if it's physically unheard.'

'I imagine that's what you believe about us; that we can somehow continue to exist when we are invisible, like Beethoven's experience of music.'

Sheila was surprised that the Professor was almost inviting a conversation about the great mystery of what is actually real. Perhaps some of Bertie's philosophy was finally rubbing off on him.

Later, in thinking more about Beethoven and his music, she realised that it was the same with voices, familiar voices. You can hear them in your head, yet there is no actual sound; no need for ears.

After Sheila had left, the Professor was dimly aware that although he hadn't talked to her about what he was intending to talk about – like alternative ways to tackle his cancer – their conversation, and the game they had briefly played together, had stirred up some unusual thoughts.

No, not thoughts, he then decided, as he slowly and in some pain climbed the stairs to bed. What was the word he was looking for? 'Maybe there isn't such a word, you poor old man,' he whispered to himself.

CHAPTER SEVENTEEN

*In which the Professor's imagination is tested,
and Peggy has a visitor.*

———— • —————— • ————

The following morning Bertie called round to see the Professor and found him in good spirits. They talked about Peggy's discovery and how suddenly there was a real possibility that the plan for a bypass might be abandoned.

Bertie sensed, however, that the Professor was just making conversation and that, not surprisingly, he had other things on his mind. After a pause – the sort of pause that comes quite naturally between two people who know each other well – the Professor said, 'It's hard to imagine what death will be like.'

Bertie nodded and waited, guessing that his friend had more to say.

'I suppose if we're dead there's nothing left of us to experience anything – life, death and certainly not snails or books.'

Another pause. Bertie gave his friend's arm a squeeze and nodded, but more in sympathy than in agreement.

'Anyway that's what I've always thought,' the Professor went on, 'as much as I've ever thought about that sort of thing. But now … well, things are a bit different. It's all rather immediate. Can you imagine what it's like to die, Bertie? Do you just fall asleep and that's it? No more dawns … no more breakfasts.'

'Imagination is an extraordinary thing,' said Bertie, 'but like everything else in life it seems to have its limitations; and understanding death certainly seems to be one of those limitations. By the way, I've just been reading an essay by an American philosopher which has the title "What Is It Like to Be a Bat?"'

'That's quite a challenge for the imagination!'

'Certainly, and that's why I'm mentioning it. Our first reaction to such a question, the author suggests, is to think it must be rather boring to hang upside down in the dark and eat flies!'

'If I was going to be awake in the night I'd rather be an owl than a bat,' responded the Professor, whose first instinct still was to bring any metaphysical discussion to a quick halt. 'At least as an owl you can see something,' he added with a smile.

'Yes, but what the writer goes on to say in his essay is that the really important and challenging question is "What is it like for a *bat* to be a bat?"'

'Go on.'

'Well, what he's getting at are the limits to our imagination, which is why I'm telling you about it; he's also drawing attention to our narrow and subjective response to everything. We're not very good at putting ourselves into the shoes of another person, let alone a bat.'

The Professor nodded, but said nothing. Bertie took the nod as a sign that his friend was starting to take an interest, and felt encouraged to continue.

'So to imagine an existence beyond death is almost impossible as long as we think of it in wholly human and subjective terms. We have a body with eyes and ears, arms and legs, and we experience ourselves as being essentially separate – certainly physically separate – from everyone and everything else. How could there possibly be an existence that's not like that?'

'That's *my* question,' said the Professor. 'What's his name, this American?'

'Thomas Nagel.'

'Never heard of him.'

'Why should you, if you don't read philosophy? I struggle with it myself – usually too abstract and clever for me – but I've found his essay has been helpful to my recognising what could be an important first step in our capacity to imagine and experience, for example, what it's like to be another person – to be Peggy, to be Bunny, even to be Joey, who in one sense knows so little and yet is so alive.'

'I suppose it's what's called empathy that you're talking about. I was talking to Sheila about empathy only yesterday.'

'It's exactly that; and perhaps from another perspective, at another level, it could also gradually lead to understanding, and above all to experiencing, not only what it might be like to be a bat, but gradually what a purely spiritual existence, outside of time and space, might also be like – an existence that not only kicks in when we die, but can and does permeate our day-to-day life, but largely unconsciously.'

The Professor frowned, and Bertie could see that all this was starting to be too much for his friend. He would like to have shared with him what he was increasingly finding so interesting in certain mystical traditions: namely that part of our experience after death – and by implication also during sleep – is that we cease to be mere onlookers and instead really do step into the shoes of a bat, a tree, a sparrow and everything else that we have previously experienced from the outside as observers.

Instead Bertie decided to bring the conversation gently back to earth, but without totally abandoning the theme they had been exploring.

'Can I read you something that the poet Ronald Blythe wrote in his book *The Circling Year*?' I brought it along in case our conversation went in this direction. It says very clearly what I've been trying to express.'

'Go on. I met him once when I was lecturing at Cambridge. A Suffolk man, I believe; always a good sign.'

'Here's the sentence: "Our mistake has always been to have believed that our immortal life begins when our mortal life ends, when in fact these dual states of our being, the temporal and the eternal, run side by side from our birth."'

Two days after his conversation with the Professor about imagination, Bertie joined Peggy and Bunny at midday to greet the man from Buglife. Much to their relief and delight the creature on the windowsill in Peggy's porch was immediately identified as a Desmoulin's whorl snail. They then took their visitor to the place on the forest where Peggy had found it.

For about ten minutes they all hunted in vain, but finally Bunny discovered a whole colony hiding, she imagined, from the increasingly cold weather. The expert took photographs, and Peggy's tiny friend was returned to its family.

The rain-soaked trio were then told that Buglife would now report the discovery to Natural England. That body would in turn designate the site as a Special Conservation Area, alongside its already distinguished status, thus hopefully giving it strong protection from development. Natural England would also write to the Department for Transport and to Defra to express their concern about the threat this scheme posed to a colony of very rare snails.

'Is there anything that we could or should still be doing?' asked Bunny. Just because she'd started to play the piano again, she wasn't giving up on her role as warrior and activist.

'The more that people continue to write or email – in other words to squeal – the better,' was the reply. 'Keep up the pressure.'

Bertie had already contacted their MP and the local newspapers, and an online petition was collecting an increasing number of signatures. Now the discovery of these very rare snails could also be announced. Laws, both national and international, protecting the environment can always be changed, the Buglife man added, so it was important that they set things in motion as soon as possible.

Peggy thought again about contacting *The Guardian*. What was that man called … George something? Maybe he would write something about the whole saga; and as she was the regular *Guardian* reader – although she always passed on her copy to Bertie – it seemed right that she should be the one to approach him.

Meanwhile Bertie was already imagining the seasons continuing to unfold undisturbed, year after year, on their beloved forest – a forest once described by one cynical councillor he'd met as 'unused space'. But for him, and for so many others, it was a place that provided peace and inspiration and, hopefully, would continue to do so for generations to come.

With Christmas approaching, and all the extra expense involved, Sheila had spent the last few days worrying about her finances. Although outwardly cheerful and optimistic, she didn't always feel cheerful on the inside. She'd found it difficult to get any sort of job while Joey was still at home all day, but she hadn't wanted to pack him off to school to be weighed, measured and tested at too early an age.

She worried, too, about Joey being an only child. He needed the company of other children, but so far she'd been unable to find any like-minded parents. In another year he could start school, but how to manage until then was her immediate concern. At least he has some colourful adults in his life, she thought.

For a while Sheila had wondered about using her DIY skills on a professional basis, but she could never be instantly available if someone's pipes had burst or their drains were blocked. Recently she'd put an ad in the Post Office window offering herself as a painter and decorator, but so far no one had got in touch. She'd been encouraged by the fact that when the Major's electrics were giving trouble, Joey had played happily by himself while she was busy, though not too far away. True, he was even happier when the Major joined in his game.

Despite these worries, the playful, creative and more outrageous Sheila was also stirring. She always liked to make her own Christmas cards, and the ones to her family and friends in Australia needed posting by the end of the week.

Like Bertie, she also wanted to avoid clichés – no snowdrops, no holly, no Victorian skaters on a pond. In her case it was humour that she felt was needed. Recently she'd remembered a joke she'd heard years ago during a Christmas party game back home.

Q. Why didn't Mary and Joseph stay at the inn?
A. Because they wanted a stable relationship.

At least it would be different, she thought; the question on the front of the card, and the answer inside.

She also liked drawing, particularly caricatures, and had already started to do some sketches of a weary-looking couple with a donkey walking past a clapped-out hotel on the outskirts of Melbourne. Inside the card she planned a drawing of Mum, Dad, baby, donkey, three wise men and three shepherds all romping in the hay.

Would it shock the English, particularly in a place as English as Hartfield? Too bad, she thought. At least people would look at it for more than the three seconds that robins in the snow or bunches of mistletoe usually get.

And the vicar? Hopefully, he'd never see it, unless he started to look through the cards on Bunny's mantelpiece at her traditional Boxing Day drinks party.

Maybe she'd get Joey to make one or two cards for their more conservative friends like the Major and the Professor. He liked drawing stars at the moment, but she'd have to persuade him to leave out the spaceships.

Chapter Eighteen

In which everyone prepares for Christmas, and Bertie goes for a walk on his own.

———————•————•————•———————

In the week or so leading up to Christmas the Professor became much weaker, and his doctor arranged for a carer to visit morning and evening to help him cope with washing, and getting dressed and undressed, and to prepare his meals.

Bunny went to see him every day and gradually learnt what food he really enjoyed and the music he liked to listen to. She also noticed that he'd begun to enjoy the village gossip, which previously had been of little interest to him.

She would have loved to talk to him about the story by Leo Tolstoy that Bertie had recommended and she had just finished reading; but, given the circumstances, she felt it might not be appropriate. It tells how a rather disagreeable middle-aged judge, Ivan Ilych, gradually comes to terms with his terminal illness. The story kept reminding her in a milder way of the Professor's situation, and she'd found it an extraordinarily moving example of how people actually can change and grow, often in surprising ways. In Ivan's case there is a gradual shift from someone who is essentially selfish and obsessed by his own standing in the world, to a person who is increasingly distressed by the suffering that his illness is causing, not just to himself, but to others. Even his attitude to death, which initially was an exaggerated version of what the Professor himself believed – or certainly used to believe – becomes a calm acceptance. In fact Bunny felt that Tolstoy conveys in a totally credible way what becomes a mood of real serenity, in which the judge finally has an intimation that the death of the body is not the death of our existence.

The whole experience of the Professor's illness had woken fears in Bunny, not just about her friend's mortality, but also about her own. At the end of Tolstoy's story, as the family are gathered round the judge's bedside and he utters his last breath, he hears someone say, 'It is over.' The author then imagines Ivan's response: 'It is death that is over.'

Bertie, too, visited the Professor every day and found him surprisingly peaceful, and grateful to everyone for their help and concern. Though still able to walk, but only slowly and in pain, he had let Peggy do some shopping for him, knowing that it would cheer her up to feel needed. The more he thought about others in this way, the less troubled he found himself feeling about his own situation.

Bertie wound his clocks for him on Sundays and helped him to sort out his post. Several old university colleagues had sent him Christmas cards. Clearly, the word had got around that he was unwell.

Sheila, meanwhile, had some welcome news: the Major had asked her if she would take on some regular household duties for him – 'cleaning and that sort of thing', he'd mumbled. Why he suddenly wanted some order in his life was a mystery, but no more so than Bunny's return to her piano, or Peggy's confidence in writing to an important and much respected journalist.

Having spent three days mucking out the Major, Sheila went off to Brighton for the day with Joey to see Father Christmas, the dolphins and, most importantly, the sea. Out there, and not that far away, Joey liked to imagine Australia and kangaroos, and also that nice man who sometimes sent them presents.

Bouncer, too, felt comfortable about splashing out as the celebrations drew near, having heard that he'd landed a part in a new play, scheduled to start rehearsals in January. Initially it would be on tour, but, as the author was already successful, there was a good chance of it ending up in the West End. He was keen to buy Sheila, and not just Joey, something special for Christmas and was also wondering what might please the Professor.

Over the road, Peggy was busy with her pipe cleaners, making rather skinny-looking angels to send to Devon; and Bertie had finished his poem about the legend of the stork.

Over the years, Christmas Eve had become the most special time of the year for Bertie. He liked to spend the day alone and on the forest. When it started to get dark he would call by for tea with Peggy.

The previous day he'd received a long letter from his old friend, Christopher, which had set him wondering about friendship and about how one learns from all sorts of different people at various stages in one's life. At one time he'd rather looked up to his friend as a teacher of sorts; certainly someone who, being slightly older, knew more about the world and had read books that he had yet to discover.

As Bertie sat on a bench near the clump of pine trees where they'd often talked, he remembered their conversations about the various characters in the village and their different foibles – Bunny's busyness, the Major's gloom, Peggy's nervousness. Perhaps Christopher would be surprised to meet them now. In some ways they were still much the same, and yet from time to time, and like most other people, they revealed a lot more when they felt safe to drop their masks.

The potential problem with relationships, thought Bertie, particularly close ones, is that people tend to trap one another within their image of that person, and so comes the feeling that they know exactly what their friend is going to say next or how each of them will react in a new situation. They're usually right, he acknowledged to himself, but even if the feelings are ones of affection, born out of long years of familiarity, this state of affairs can put an unspoken dampener on someone actually saying or doing something different, something new.

Certainly Bertie had been surprised by Bunny's recent hunger for what she called deeper conversations. Perhaps her initial hostility to Bouncer, and her subsequent shame at some of her prejudices, had been the awakener. The Major's response to a small child invading his space had been another surprise. And why had Peggy finally decided to talk about her troubled past?

Eventually Bertie and Christopher had gone their separate ways – Christopher into the dizzy heights of government, Bertie into the quieter life of teaching. But although Bertie now spent much of his time on his own, he didn't feel he was what psychologists would call an introvert; he was far too fond of visiting his friends to justify that particular label. True, he wrote poetry that hardly anyone ever read, and had thoughts that seemed more and more at odds with what occupied most people.

One particular thought that increasingly occupied him was connected with the word 'eternity'. Some months ago he'd written to *The Times* about an article they'd published at Easter on the subject of the resurrection and eternal life. His letter wasn't published, but Bertie hadn't wavered in the thought he'd tried to express. For most people, he'd pointed out, the idea of eternal life implies endless time stretching on and on into the future, without end. For Bertie, however, eternity was most helpfully described centuries ago by the German mystic Johannes Tauler, in the simple phrase 'Eternity is the everlasting now'. Maybe that experience of living fully in the moment – aware of but uncluttered by either past or future – is what existence is like in sleep, and above all when we are no longer physically alive; a state in which comes a very different kind of consciousness. Eternity, therefore, has nothing to do with time.

Despite his seemingly obscure ideas and the frequent loneliness and isolation that such thoughts provoked, Bertie had no regrets about the way his life had unfolded. What had recently started to change for him was his reaction to situations that previously would have depressed him – for example, the people he sometimes saw in town who looked totally overwhelmed and defeated by life. Last week he had noticed a man sitting alone on a bench in his slippers, clearly in no hurry. He was probably there, thought Bertie, because he had nothing else to do and nowhere welcoming to go, whereas on his bench in the centre of town he was at least in company, even though everyone passed him by. What Bertie then imagined was that if he, Bertie, were suddenly to drop down on the pavement with a heart attack, this man – along with many of those other seemingly sad and vulnerable people – would be kind and helpful.

He knew that some of the villagers saw him as a little naïve. A 'crank' was how someone had described him, so Bunny had told him with a smile. What immediately came to mind, and cheered him up immensely, was a description he'd recently read of cranks as 'small, useful, and inexpensive tools that make revolutions'.

Above all Bertie believed increasingly in the essential goodness in people, and he trusted in a wisdom that made sure that whatever each person meets in life, however challenging, is appropriate to their deep inner needs. Whatever he, Bertie, has had to learn is different from whatever it is that Christopher is learning.

Bertie sometimes thought he should have been a monk, but, since he didn't like the idea of being tied down to anything, least of all a belief system, he knew that would never have worked. In fact he was increasingly suspicious of any kind of certainty, whether religious or scientific. It wasn't because he believed that human beings could never know the truth, but rather because he was aware what limited creatures we still are, despite being able to make aeroplanes and compose music, write poetry and solve algebraic equations. In this light he liked some words of the painter John Constable – 'We see nothing truly until we understand it' – and had written them down in a 'Book of Thoughts' that he kept by his bed.

'How much we must be missing!' was Bertie's reaction on first reading that quotation. But perhaps our greatest ability, he sometimes thought, is to recognise our failings and yet have faith in our unfulfilled potential – the potential that he'd talked about to Bunny.

Recently, since his bees had gone to sleep for the winter, he'd been thinking more about the moon and how he loved to gaze at it, especially when it was full. The other night, there'd been a lot of cloud, but after a while – instead of feeling frustrated at only occasionally getting a glimpse of his great, glowing friend – he began to look at and appreciate the clouds. Was his obsession with always wanting to see the moon, and just the moon, the same problem as having some fixed idea and image of God? We tend not to look at everything else that might in fact tell us just as much about that God – perhaps even more – than the picture we cling to. In their way the clouds are just as mysterious and beautiful as the moon, he had realised; so, too, are many other things that people so often take for granted as they rush from one place to another, from one sensation to the next.

If he had any religion at all, he thought, perhaps this was it. Everything in life is sacred, and in their interdependence – bees and flowers, trees and sunlight, wind and rain – things are not just individual manifestations of the divine, but in their totality are Divinity itself. This, he liked to think, is the ecology towards which he and many others are slowly moving; an ecology that embraces both nature and the heavens; and alongside this awareness the recognition of a universe that is for us part visible, part hidden.

And we human beings, where do we fit in? We, too, thought Bertie, depend on everything else and on each other, but maybe we have the added challenge of taking evolution further. It was another thought that he'd tried to share with Bunny some weeks ago. She hadn't started to read Hegel as a result, but at least she was playing the piano again.

Such deep mysteries were eventually inclined to set even Bertie's head spinning. On this occasion he was soothed by the thought of Peggy's fireside, a cup of tea and a warm crumpet – maybe two.

CHAPTER NINETEEN

In which the Major almost enjoys himself,
and Peggy triumphs at poker.

———————◆———◆———————

That Christmas in Hartfield, if it had been observed by an outsider, would have seemed much the same as any year. Yet if you peeled away the carols and presents and feasting, then nothing was the same. 'Nothing in life, if truly alive, stays still' was one of Bertie's sayings. Every moment is unique, and not just at Christmas; and so it was in Hartfield.

The Major had never before had Christmas lunch with an actor, a noisy and excited six-year-old and a woman who stuffed her turkey with gooseberries and dried marijuana.

Peggy and Bertie spent the day with the Professor who in previous years had treated Christmas as an inconvenient distraction, involving shops closed for days, cards from people he could hardly remember, and carol singers ringing on his doorbell while he was trying to work.

Peggy had prepared a splendid meal with Bertie's help, and in the afternoon, after Bertie read to the others his poem about the legend of the stork, all three of them fell asleep. Later the Professor taught them how to play poker. As a child Peggy had only ever played snap. She remembered always losing.

After church, Bunny went to her usual family gathering for Christmas lunch, but was a much quieter, thoughtful member of the party than in previous years. Later she went round to see the Professor and found Peggy decidedly tipsy, having won three games of poker in a row.

Back at Sheila's the Major was, for the first time in his life, enjoying a flamboyant display of charades, though strictly as a spectator. The highlight was Bouncer as a snail being examined and measured by Joey as the expert. Sheila then did a wonderful imitation of Bunny trying to play the piano while on the phone to the leader of the East Sussex County Council.

As Bertie walked home alone, having gently steered Peggy back to her cottage, he wondered what lay ahead for them all in the coming year. He also wondered whether those tiny snails would really be important and powerful enough to stop the bulldozers.

By the middle of January, Peggy was longing to contact Buglife for news, but both Bunny and Bertie advised her not to hassle her contact and to trust that the campaign was underway, with bits of paper and forms and emails finding their way from one office to another, from one bureaucrat to the next.

A few weeks later, Bunny drove Peggy, Bertie and Sheila to Watford to see Bouncer in his new play. The Major had volunteered to look after Joey for the day. As the matinee would be over by five o'clock, they promised to try to be back by Joey's bedtime.

They all found it intriguing to see someone they knew well taking part in a story that had nothing to do with any of them. Bouncer had a serious role – as a villain, in fact – so none of his playfulness and humour that they knew so well was apparent.

'How strange to be someone else!' was Peggy's overriding thought as she sat gazing at the stage. Perhaps we would all benefit from doing that from time to time. She even wondered about approaching Bunny for a role in the village entertainment that was being devised for Valentine's Day next year. Maybe they would let her play the villain and not typecast her as a timid little woman. Bertie had once suggested that there was a villain in all of us. Let's find it, thought Peggy.

By now her mind had wandered so far that she'd lost track of the play. Why was Bouncer's character suddenly so upset and shouting at his wife? Why was Bunny suddenly looking at her programme and not at the stage? Why were the couple in front of her talking? There was a lot to be said for quietly reading a book on one's own by the fireside, she thought. And why was Bouncer now suddenly in tears? Maybe she did need that hearing aid that Sheila had tactfully suggested some months ago. Hopefully, Bertie would fill in the gaps for her during the interval.

They went round to Bouncer's dressing room after the show, and Peggy felt very important. They all agreed what a pity it was that the Professor was too unwell to be with them. On the journey back to Sussex, despite the excitement of the outing, they all felt in their different ways how fortunate they were to live in a small village surrounded by beautiful countryside. But Sheila and Bertie, in particular, also felt how important it was to stay connected to what people call 'the real world', and not to let their privileged lives insulate them from it.

By the time they started to notice more trees than houses, each one of the party was enjoying the silence that allowed them to quietly dwell in their private world of thoughts, memories and hopes. Joey was asleep when they finally got home; so, too, in Sheila's large and comfortable armchair, was the Major.

Bunny's New Year resolution had been to put her weight behind Peggy's failed initiative to start a Book Club. Both of them were determined to include in the group some men, who for some reason seemed to avoid such gatherings. They'd been warned that men tend to hog discussions, but felt quite confident they could crush any such displays of male superiority.

Bertie happily agreed to join, as did Sheila and Bouncer. Bunny also felt that it would be a good opportunity to talk together about something other than snails and planning regulations. It was agreed that Peggy would choose the first book. What had caught her eye about the one she settled on was a review that praised the author's skill in demonstrating how happiness can emerge from great suffering. The setting of *The Life of an Unknown Man* by Andrei Makine was twentieth-century Russia, but Peggy knew – despite her sheltered life – that people are essentially much the same, whether in Moscow or Hartfield, Siberia or North Devon.

On the day after the first meeting of the Book Club, the Professor was moved into the local hospice. His friends had continued to visit him daily, but his situation had become such that he needed specialised care and managed pain relief day and night.

Before he left he wrote a note to Sheila thanking her for their conversations and saying that he'd been doing some remembering. The phrase that had kept coming into his head from Sundays long ago was 'I will lift up mine eyes unto the hills from whence cometh my help'.

His serenity amazed everyone, and it became obvious to most people, whether so-called believers or not, that although his body was clearly dying, his spirit – that essence in him that had expressed itself in this lifetime as an academic, a bachelor and a rationalist – was well and strong. For Bunny, in particular, it was clear evidence of what her conversations with Bertie had stirred in her: namely that there is something in every person which is really quite independent of the body.

Another big change in Peggy's life came about through a chance conversation with the head teacher of the local primary school, who, because of cuts to her budget, was having problems giving extra help to several of the children who had difficulties with their lessons. Aware of her own struggles at school, Peggy suddenly felt a huge surge of sympathy for the two or three children the teacher was describing. What emerged from their conversation was how helpful it would be if Peggy could spend an afternoon every week seeing each of these children individually, primarily to help with their reading.

Peggy remembered how important books were to her as a child – a wonderful escape from the trials of having to deal with real people. In fact the characters in those stories had been just as real to her: wise friends who helped her to cope not only with the sticks and stones of childhood, but also with the frequent teasing and spiteful words.

Sheila's life also took a surprising turn in the New Year. It started with her offer to mend the vicar's bicycle, which she'd found abandoned outside the Post Office. Through conversations that followed she decided to enrol Joey in a twice-weekly playgroup hosted at the vicarage. Then it wasn't long before the radical and outspoken Aussie – the woman who not only called a spade a spade but would also refer to a wallaby as a 'bloody wallaby' – was taking her little angel to the Sunday morning's Children's Service that preceded Matins.

Meanwhile, in those early weeks of the New Year, something had happened to Bertie which had troubled him deeply. In a letter he received from a complete stranger – someone who'd read his poem in the parish magazine about the stork bringing the newborn baby – he was accused of living in a fantasy world and ignoring what matters to most ordinary people.

Why did the letter upset him so much? True, the tone was aggressive, but nonetheless what the writer was expressing struck a chord, a raw nerve, despite the fact that he, Bertie, appeared to the world to be so serene and self-assured.

On and off for years, he had asked himself this same old question. What's the point of lofty ideas and philosophical speculations when so many people, millions of people, had little education, or not enough to eat, or were punished for not conforming to the societies in which they lived? His life was safe and secure, his pension arrived every month, his roof didn't leak, and he could eat as many chocolate biscuits as he liked. He would then tell himself that he was too old to go and work in an African orphanage or glue himself to the railings round Parliament.

He also recognised and understood that most people's lack of interest in what so fascinated him was not because they were thoughtless or insensitive. What life had taught him over the years was that many of his fellow human beings – like that man on the bench in town – were simply too preoccupied with coping from day to day to have time for such reflections. When they did start to put aside their own immediate problems, what they mainly cared about was how to make *this* world a better place, rather than dwelling on some imagined heaven elsewhere.

Bertie felt, however, that this shift in people's consciousness and priorities towards the needs and sufferings of others was encouraging and necessary. Religion in its traditional form could too easily become an excuse to ignore the challenges of living in the here and now, of learning from it and of thinking for ourselves. It interested him, therefore, that more and more people described themselves as spiritual rather than religious.

Yet in time, so he believed, there will be a need to contemplate again the great mysteries of existence that all religions have addressed, if we are truly to progress in understanding ourselves and all that surrounds us; and, hopefully, we will do so with the intelligence and compassion that we are slowly forging from day to day here on earth.

Above all Bertie had an underlying faith in people's capacity to imagine, to laugh and to be creative, as powerful means to keep at bay all those trends in the world that conspire to turn us into earth-bound robots. And creativity, he recognised, is not just about writing poetry, composing music or painting pictures; it's also about how we choose to live our lives.

Recently he had also begun to sense, or at least to hope, that the things we feel and think – our ideas, thoughts and prayers – even if they seem never to be heard or read – can nevertheless have a healing power in the world at large. Thus, whenever the World Wide Web was mentioned, he often imagined its spiritual equivalent – no electronic gadgets, but something far more complex and miraculous: a source of helpful and inspiring information and insights that are constantly available if we press the right invisible buttons.

With all these thoughts bubbling away in his mind, Bertie's New Year resolution had been to finally start work on the book that he had long been planning. He still only had a rough outline in his head, but he sensed that the details would emerge as he gave it his full attention. His idea was prompted by Plato's allegory of the cave, in which he has Socrates describe a group of people who have lived chained to the wall of a cave all their lives. For them reality is the shadows on the wall created by objects passing in front of a fire behind them. Whether this was the situation in which people still largely lived was the question that interested Bertie. As he saw it – and he presumed this was what Plato was saying – our challenge is to turn round, and not just physically but in our minds, and to see what's creating those shadows.

Above all, as he set to work on his book, Bertie had the conviction that whatever it is that is causing the shadows that people take for reality, this mystery is deeply connected to what we respect and value in the here and now; and so to care about bees and snails, and about other people, is as sacred an act as kneeling down on Sundays and singing hymns to whatever it is that created these miracles.

It was towards the end of March that another miracle occurred, alongside the miracle that greeted Bertie and his friends every year with the coming of spring – in his case the appearance of masses of dandelions on his garden path and the blossom on his two apple trees.

The news came from three different directions, all within one week. Peggy received a call from Buglife, Bertie had another handwritten note from Christopher, and Bunny had an email from her planning inspector friend. Plans for a bypass across the Ashdown Forest had been shelved.

It wasn't clear, and perhaps never would be, what the deciding factor was. The discovery of the snails was probably significant, along with the efforts of various other conservation bodies; so, too, the enormous number of signatures to the online petition, and maybe the article that appeared in *The Guardian* just after Christmas. Perhaps in the end Sir Christopher had indeed pulled a few strings in Whitehall, but in his note to Bertie there was no mention of such a thing, only jubilation.

And it was with jubilation that Bunny called a celebratory meeting of the Action Group – with tea and biscuits, and a bubbly treat that she knew would quickly turn Peggy's cheeks very pink.

Chapter Twenty

*In which good news is eclipsed by bad,
and the battle continues.*

———————

'I've been to see the Professor to tell him the good news,' said Bunny to the assembled group, 'but I didn't mention the bad bit.'

Everyone had assembled for the celebratory meeting, except the Major.

'Where is he?' asked Bouncer.

'Should you phone him?' suggested Peggy.

'I have, and left a message,' replied Bunny. 'He's probably on his way.'

'I wonder what he'll make of this latest bombshell?' said a dejected-looking Sheila.

'"I told you so," or something like that,' suggested Bouncer. 'It's sad that, despite showing occasional signs of what could be described as cheerfulness, he still seems to think that the world is basically going down the plughole and we're all doomed.'

'Perhaps we are,' said Peggy. She, more than anyone else, had been devastated by the news that had arrived just a few days after the announcement that plans for a Hartfield Bypass had been abandoned.

Bertie was determined to be optimistic, but in his heart was also deeply troubled by this latest development.

'Clearly,' he volunteered, 'our work together isn't over.'

'Or ever will be, if you ask me,' chipped in an unusually deflated Bunny.

'It's not the end of the world,' continued Bertie. 'It's only in fairy stories that people live happily ever after. Perhaps one day we will, but I suspect that's a long way down the road. More dragons to slay. More damsels in distress to rescue.'

'Are you suggesting that the forest is one of those damsels?' asked Bouncer with a smile. He, too, was keen to avoid a retreat into total despondency.

'Certainly,' said Bertie, 'and the forest is not alone. The soil, the trees, even water – they are all vulnerable and under threat as long as we human beings continue to believe in our superior intelligence and in our right to manipulate and control things for our own selfish needs.'

'So what do we do?' asked Sheila. 'Do we need to be bolder in our response? Go on hunger strike? Go to prison?'

'Or simply say our prayers?' suggested Bunny.

The others were surprised to hear a remark like that from the busy and ever-practical organiser of so many down-to-earth initiatives.

'Yes,' said Bertie, 'but prayer coupled with action.'

'If you ask me,' said Bouncer, 'I have a hunch that what goes on in these thick heads of ours, including prayer, has a lot more clout in the scheme of things than we realise.'

'I'd go even further,' added Bertie; 'or put it another way: what we think today will, in all likelihood, be the reality of tomorrow.'

After a long pause during which each one of them tried to digest the implications of Bertie's statement, the sound of Bunny's doves taking off for their morning flight reminded them that life goes on, whatever nonsense human beings think or get up to. It was Bouncer who finally broke the silence.

'Maybe at another level there really is a wise, mysterious and helping hand at work.'

'Are we talking about God?' asked Peggy.

'I suppose some would call it God,' replied Bertie. 'Bouncer's thought certainly implies the existence of what I think of as a wiser realm than our own.'

'But what I don't understand', said Bunny, 'is why this wise and all-powerful God, if he does exist, allows us to make such a mess of things? Some say we're on course to destroy not only all life on earth, but the planet itself.'

'That's the great mystery,' replied Bertie. 'Perhaps God is not all-powerful; and maybe he, too, has enemies.'

'You mean the devil?' said Peggy.

'I suppose that's what I do mean,' replied Bertie. 'But in answer to Bunny's question about – what did you call it? – "the mess we make of things" – if we *are* in some way the children of this God, then maybe, like all good parents, that great mystery that created us wants us to grow up, become adults, stand on our own two feet, think for ourselves, even to rebel, and then perhaps to take things further. But to do that we have to be free to make mistakes, otherwise we'd just be puppets on strings.'

Silence again. No sign of the doves. The church clock struck the half-hour. In the distance the sound of a barking dog was suddenly drowned by some passing cars. Peggy started to wonder what her little snail was feeling.

This time it was Sheila who finally spoke: '"God has no hands but ours" is what my Dad used to say.'

At that moment the telephone rang. The Major had muddled up the time of the meeting.

'Are you coming?' asked Bunny. She rolled her eyes as that familiar, lugubrious voice responded. 'And have you seen the local paper?' she asked. 'No?

It's on the front page: an article about Disney. They want to buy the Ashdown Forest to build a theme park.'

    A pause while the Major reacted to the news.

    'What?' said Bunny.

    Another pause.

    'Yes, I imagine there will be donkey rides.'

Bertie's poem to mark the relaunch of the Action Group

There is a forest near our homes
where people like to walk;
and we will never save it
if all we do is talk.

It's also home to Pooh and Roo,
to Piglet and an owl.
We may not see them with our eyes,
or hear them when they howl,

but they exist, and always will,
just like the clouds and trees;
for stories that we know and love
are precious as my bees.

But some just see this open space
as lacking any fun,
with nettles, mud and rabbit holes –
all hazards people shun.

So we must fight with wit and nerve,
not swayed by each new pound;
nor yield to plastic, froth and fakes,
or concrete on the ground.

Below our feet, and in the air
are treasures that we need;
but if we hack and blast and spray
they'll die through human greed.

POSTSCRIPT

At his request, the Professor's legacy to his old college was used to establish a Research Fellowship for the study of invertebrates.

At Joey's christening the Major became his godfather and wore a suit for the occasion.

After a brief affair with the vicar, Sheila returned to Australia with Joey and trained as a Jungian analyst. In the years to come she was proud to witness her son become a distinguished entomologist.

Bouncer and Bunny's production of *Heartaches in Hartfield*, after its premiere in the Village Hall, went on to become a hit in the West End and later on Broadway.

After two years' work at the local school, Peggy took a degree in Child Development at the Open University and was later awarded an MBE for her charitable work with vulnerable children.

Bunny bought a bicycle and joined the Quakers. She also tried to ensure that the Major improved his diet by eating the occasional raw carrot.

Bertie's book, *The Shadows*, won a prestigious First Novel award. He also became a prison visitor and eventually gave up chocolate biscuits.

The government blocked the East Sussex County Council's sale of the Ashdown Forest to the Disney Corporation, and the Demoulin's whorl snails continued to live there in peace, undisturbed by roads or roller coasters and seldom noticed by people in awe of the birds and the deer, the heather and gorse, the trees and wild flowers.

Yet all these more conspicuous miracles depended in their different ways *on* those snails, and on the ants and the spiders, the frogs and the beetles and a hundred other tiny creatures that between them helped to create and sustain that enchanted place that Bertie and his friends so loved.

By the same author, an autobiography
published by Hawthorn Press in 2009
ISBN 978-1-903458-90-7 Hardback 592 pages

'A deeply thoughtful book, the result of a lifetime of thinking, reading, and conversations with an amazing cast of people' – Mark Tully.

'Jonathan Stedall brings the same sensitivity and spiritual insight to the printed page that he brought to his many television documentaries' – Theodore Roszak.

'A wonderfully written book, with much insight, tenderness, and candour' – Arthur Zajonc.

'A real quest, with outward work perfectly integrated with an inner search' – Karen Armstrong.

'A thoughtful book by a thoughtful man' – Ben Okri.

By the same author, meditations on death, bereavement and hope
published by Hawthorn Press in 2017
ISBN 978-1-907359-81-1 Hardback 160 pages

'The poems are beautiful, poignant and inspiring' – Stephen Gawtry, Managing Editor, Watkins Mind Body Spirit.

'It sounds odd to say of such a profound book, rather than a thriller, but I couldn't put it down. The poems are beautiful - simple, clear, honest, moving' – Craig Brown, critic and satirist.

'These are honest poems, without pretension, that marry deep feeling and thoughtfulness, opening us towards a sense (so difficult to articulate) of another level of reality' – Jeremy Naydler, author of Goethe on Science and Gardening as a Sacred Art.

ORDERING BOOKS

If you have difficulties ordering Hawthorn Press books from a bookshop, you can order direct from our website www.hawthornpress.com, or from our UK distributor: BookSource, 50 Cambuslang Road, Glasgow, G32 8NB
Tel: (0845) 370 0063, Email: orders@booksource.net
Details of our overseas distributors can be found on our website.

Hawthorn Press
www.hawthornpress.com